Jennifer Torres

the
WIN OVER

the WIN OVER

Jennifer Torres

Scholastic Press / New York

To my tías with love and gratitude

Library of Congress Cataloging-in-Publication Data available

ISBN 978-1-338-81890-1

10 9 8 7 6 5 4 3 2 1   23 24 25 26 27

Printed in Italy   183

First edition, February 2023

Book design by Stephanie Yang

1

At first Lucinda Mendoza thought her sister was exaggerating. Raquel could be a little dramatic that way. But maybe it was true. Maybe there *weren't* any stories worth digging into at Dad's house in the middle of California farmland. Was that really such a bad thing? Wasn't the calm kind of ... nice? Especially after months of chaos.

Lucinda sat on the grass, her legs stretched in a wide V. She leaned over the left leg, reaching for her toe, and watched Juliette dip a white T-shirt, its front a constellation of knots and rubber bands, into a bucket of bright pink water.

Raquel, Lucinda's twin, knelt next to Jules, notebook open to a clean, blank page, pen raised and ready to make note of anything that happened. Anything at all.

Nothing did.

Jules swirled the shirt in the water with a stick she had pulled off one of the oak trees that Dad's small ranch, Los Robles, was named for. "I'm not sure how long it's supposed to sit in there," she said, frowning into the punch-colored stew.

Raquel peeked over the edge of the bucket. "Let's start with a few questions while we wait," she said. She tapped her pen against her teeth. "What gave you the idea to tie-dye your clothes in beet juice in the first place? Is it a *trend*? Are kids our age trying to get back to the basics? Reviving old-school, all-natural techniques? Giving up fast fashion?"

She sat up on her knees. Her eyes glimmered. Lucinda recognized the flash of a new idea.

"That could be a great angle, actually," Raquel continued, scribbling furiously into her notebook. "Are you doing this . . . beet juice thing . . . for environmental reasons?" She inched closer to Jules. "To make your own clothes and take action against a system that creates millions of tons of textile waste each year?"

This was getting desperate, even for Raquel, who, as editor of their school news site, the *Manzanita Mirror*, charged toward stories with a stubborn persistence that could be a little intimidating if you weren't used to it. Lucinda met Jules's nervous glance, rolled her eyes, and stretched over the other leg.

"I *guess*?" Jules answered finally. "I mean, honestly, I just thought it would be cool to see how it would turn out. Since we have all those beets and everything. I didn't want them to go to waste. That's good for the environment, right? Reducing waste?"

Lucinda laughed, her brown curls tumbling into her face.

Raquel slumped and tossed her notebook and pen beside her.

"Don't be mad," Jules said, her cheeks turning as red as the beet water. "I *do* care about the environment. It's just that I didn't know all that stuff you were talking about. Let me read about it tonight, then we can do the interview tomorrow."

Raquel pulled a clump of crabgrass out of the dirt. "That's not how it works," she said. "I have to *find* a story, not create one." She raised her eyes and shrugged. "But I'm not mad. And even if it's not a story, this is fun to watch."

Jules's shoulders relaxed. The nervous lines between her eyebrows disappeared. She reached into the bucket and lifted out the shirt. It emerged, dripping, a vibrant flamingo pink. She held it up with a squeal of surprised delight, not seeming to mind that it was staining her fingers.

"Whoa!" Raquel exclaimed, whipping out her phone and snapping a picture.

"I love that color!" Lucinda added. And she meant it. "Maybe you can do one of my headbands next. Or my laces! I've always wanted to have ice skates with pink laces."

Juliette smiled and wrung out the shirt over the bucket. She took it to the laundry line that was strung across the patio and clipped it up with two clothespins to dry. She took down one of Dad's white T-shirts.

"How do you think Marcos would like a tie-dyed shirt?" she asked, her eyebrow arched.

"Do it!" Lucinda said. "He'd look great in pink."

Jules held the shirt out in front of her and tilted her head. "Nah, on second thought, I think I'll wait and make another batch with black beans," she said. "Or onion skins. I heard you can get a nice golden yellow with onion skins."

"First beets, now black beans and onions?" Raquel said. "It sounds like you're working on a chili recipe, not tie-dyeing clothes. Will you be able to get the smell out?"

Lucinda coughed to disguise a giggle. She knew Raquel was joking, but she wasn't sure Jules did. It had been almost four months since Jules and her mom, Sylvia, had moved into Dad's ranch house. After a rough beginning, the girls, all about to start seventh grade, were closer than they had been at first. They trusted one another. Mostly.

But other times, Lucinda thought, it felt like they were

still stuck back in that old nervous getting-to-know-you stage.

She didn't want Jules to think they were laughing *at* her.

And yet, she couldn't help but agree with Raquel on this one.

"Seriously, Jules," she said. "It seems like a project our mom would cook up."

"Where do you think I got the idea?" Jules said, twisting rubber bands around a pair of long gym socks. "When I messaged her to say I was going to try it, she gave me that tip about using vinegar to help set the dye. I miss your mom. She's the only one who really *got* me." Jules sighed and pressed the back of her hand to her forehead in pretend despair.

Of all the things that had changed over the past months—and so much had—Lucinda thought that Mom starting a web series was probably the most surprising.

Last spring, when it felt like the whole world stopped to slow the spread of a new virus, Mom and Dad had thought it would be safer for Lucinda and Raquel to spend the lockdown at Dad's ranch in the country rather than at Mom's apartment in busy Los Angeles. Lucinda hadn't wanted to go at first. Hadn't wanted to leave behind their home, their neighborhood—and especially not the ice rink. But Raquel had talked her into it. Like she always did. They had thought that if they convinced Mom to stay there, too, it would be a chance to bring their parents closer together again.

Until they discovered that Dad's girlfriend, Sylvia, and her daughter, Juliette, were already living at the ranch.

Lucinda's stomach still tightened when she thought about the whole mess and what a disaster it could have become—and almost did. But now, just as the world seemed to be settling into a new kind of normal, so was her family.

Well, as normal as they ever were.

Away from LA for the summer, Raquel was supposed to be taking a break from the journalism club. Yet she was still as determined as ever to find a good story.

Jules was back to practicing with her track team three days a week. And even though their sports were different, she made a great training partner. Every morning, she and Lucinda met before breakfast to jog around the ranch.

And Mom had started her web series. It was Sylvia's idea, actually, which was a little strange to think about. Sylvia worked at a marketing agency and told Mom that, with all the salons closed, people would love to see videos featuring her at-home haircut tips. She was right. People did. Tens of thousands of people. Since then, Mom had expanded the series with tutorials on some of her favorite DIY projects. Like "Clean-Out-Your-Kitchen Tie-Dye."

The projects didn't always turn out the way Mom planned, but that only seemed to make people even more excited to click on her videos. *And* more excited to book an appointment with her at the salon. She had a little extra money now and was using some of it to pay for an advanced hairstyling course in New York. That's why everyone thought it was a good idea for Lucinda and Raquel to stay up in Lockeford full-time while school was out.

At least it was *partly* why. There was also the other big change. The *biggest* change. Dad and Sylvia were getting married. They had decided during those months of shut-downs and stay-at-home orders that they worked best as a team. It had been fast, but as Sylvia said, "What's the point of waiting around when you're sure?"

She and Raquel were alike in ways that sometimes made Lucinda nervous.

This summer, before Lucinda and Raquel went back to LA to start school, was supposed to be their opportunity to be together, as a new family.

Lucinda didn't mind. There was an ice rink in Stockton, not too far from Dad's ranch, and he drove her to practice there the first day it reopened. She had even joined a syn-chronized skating team after Sylvia brought home a flyer. Her agency had designed it.

Lucinda had never been on a real team before. During the school year, Raquel had talked her into joining the journalism club, but skating was different. Skating was hers.

Lucinda stood and dusted the dirt and grass off her leg-gings. She tightened the sweatshirt she wore around her waist and glanced at Raquel.

She seemed calm, her pen tucked behind her ear as she gazed out toward the orange trees. Nevertheless, Lucinda could tell her sister's mind was whirring.

Raquel had been less than excited about the two of them spending a whole summer up in Lockeford. She swore it wasn't about the wedding—and Lucinda *almost* believed that was true—but about taking so much time away from the *Mirror*.

A lump of guilt rose in Lucinda's throat. *She* was the one who'd promised Raquel everything would work out.

"Hey, what about that story idea you had the other day?" Lucinda asked, twisting her hair into a new bun. "About endangered animals living on the farms up here?"

"Riparian brush rabbits," Raquel said. "And not on the farms. But some people have reported sightings in the woods around the river."

"That's something I've actually heard about," Jules said. "The vet at the animal shelter mentioned it. I'd go on a hike with you to take a look."

"Let's *all* go," Lucinda suggested. "This weekend, maybe. After practice."

"Really?" Raquel asked, eyes brightening again. "That'd be great. I'll look up some spots."

Then Juliette's phone pinged. She stopped stirring the dye to check it.

"It's my mom," she said. "She's asking if one of us can go help her and Marcos at the farm stand."

2

Jules looked up from her phone screen, then down at the bucket of beet water and the mound of clothes on the ground, still waiting to be dyed.

"Could one of you go this time?" she asked. "I'm . . . kind of in the middle of all this."

Lu locked her fingers and stretched her arms over her head. "Sorry," she said. "The team's going to that climbing wall that just reopened. Lina's mom is picking me up any second."

Raquel used to think ice skating took up too much of

Lu's time before, from the minutes she spent with her eyes closed, rehearsing her routines in her head, to the hours out on Mom's balcony, stretching on a yoga mat. But now, ever since she'd joined that team—which was Sylvia's idea, of *course*—it was as if skating had taken over her entire life. Lu had always struggled to get out of bed on time, but now she was awake as soon as the sun rose to jog around the ranch with Jules. Before the team, Raquel could count on Lucinda being around most of the time, but suddenly, her calendar was filled. Pool parties and outdoor movie nights and barbecues in someone's backyard. Actual *practice* seemed like an afterthought.

"What does rock climbing even have to do with figure skating anyway?" Raquel asked, flicking a pebble across the grass. Lu blinked, almost wobbling off-balance, when it bounced off her shoe. "Isn't it, like, an entirely different sport? Or is synchronized rock climbing some kind of new sport you're trying to start? Because *that* would make a great story."

Jules smirked. Lu dropped her arms and kicked the pebble back at Raquel. "Very funny," she said. "Being a team isn't all about the game, you know. It's about the experiences you have together."

Lu had been on a team for eight whole weeks, and suddenly she was an expert.

A car horn honked in front of the house.

"That's Lina," Lu said. "Gotta go." She grabbed her water bottle and mini backpack from the ground and took off jogging toward the front of the ranch house. "See you later, Jules," she called without looking back. "And sorry, Kel. We'll go on that hike, though. I promise!"

Raquel knew she meant it. But she also knew that, despite what she said, Lu would probably have other plans by the time the weekend came. Working out some new choreography with one of her teammates. Or cry-laughing over some skating joke that no one understood but them. *At least it's only for the summer*, Raquel reminded herself, not for the first time. Not even for the first time *that day*. When school started, they'd go back to Mom's apartment. Both of them.

Wouldn't they? Usually, Raquel wasn't afraid to ask tough questions. But that was one question she swept back to a dark, distant corner of her mind every time it crept into her thoughts.

The thing was, Raquel noticed things. It's what made her a good reporter. And she couldn't help but notice that Lu never talked about what would happen when the summer ended, about Dad packing their things into his truck and driving them back home to LA. She didn't make plans for catching up with their friends or even wonder about what classes they'd have.

"I guess I can go help at the farm stand," Jules said. She pushed a piece of red-brown hair out of her face, leaving a streak of beet juice on her cheek. "I'll save the rest of the clothes for when I make the black-bean dye."

Raquel sighed and lifted herself off the grass. "No, you're busy." Everyone was. "Stay—I'll go. I need a walk anyway. Maybe it'll help me come up with some new ideas."

If this were a normal summer, Raquel would have taken charge, organizing their days around Mom's schedule at the salon. She would have started in May—maybe even April—coordinating carpools with other parents, or mapping out the places they could get to on their bikes.

Printing off schedules and taping them to the fridge so everyone knew exactly where they were supposed to be, and how they were going to get there, and what they needed to bring.

But up here, Dad's schedule was the same every day, and Sylvia already kept hers in a hardcover planner that Raquel couldn't help but admire with its hour-by-hour agenda on one side and blank lines for notes on the other. Lu was even setting her own alarms every morning.

The only thing Raquel had to worry about was the one thing she had always been most sure of: The *Manzanita Mirror.* Somehow, in the midst of the pandemic and months of online learning, Raquel had managed to double the size of the newspaper staff. The special edition she edited had even won an award from the Junior Press Association.

But now that the Manzanita Middle School campus was open again, Ms. King had said the job of summer editor should go to someone who was in town. That someone turned out to be Paul Campos, a new student who had been president of the journalism club back at his old school.

Raquel hadn't been worried. At first. But when she saw the changes Paul made to the *Mirror* site, and when she read the stories he'd written, she started to wonder if Ms. King would make his summer position permanent.

Raquel had to come up with a story. Something to show Ms. King that she was still paying attention, still asking the important questions. Still the best person for the job of editor in chief. It shouldn't have been a problem. She usually had thousands of story ideas saved up, like a packet of seeds waiting to be scattered. But up here in Lockeford, she couldn't get any of them to grow.

She walked out to the farm stand at the edge of the property, reaching up and running her fingers over the waxy leaves of lemon and orange trees that Abuelo had planted before she was born. She could have found her way through them with her eyes closed, she thought. That's how well she knew Rancho Los Robles. That's how long she and Lu had been coming here.

Only, having Jules and Sylvia around made it feel like a different place. Like a favorite sweater that didn't fit the way it used to. Maybe things would *always* feel different now. Or maybe different would become normal. She wasn't sure which was better.

Raquel pulled her phone from her back pocket and dialed Mom.

She answered after two rings. She always answered.

"Kel? What's up, mija?"

There was music in the background and muffled conversation.

"You're not... with a client, are you?" Raquel pulled the phone away from her ear and checked the time. It was after seven in New York. Raquel had been sure her mom would be in her room by now.

"Momentito," Mom whispered.

When she came back a minute later, it was quieter. "Sorry about that. I just stepped into the break room so I can hear you better. Is everything all right?"

"Everything's fine," Raquel answered. Because it was, wasn't it? "Just felt like saying hi."

"I'm glad you did," Mom said. "But if there's really nothing wrong, do you mind if I give you a call a little later? A few of us stayed at the studio to practice a new coloring technique. We're just finishing up."

Even *Mom* was busy.

"Sure, of course."

"And maybe you can get your sister on, too," she continued. "It's impossible to keep up with her lately."

Raquel forced a laugh. "Yeah, she has a lot going on. Talk to you later?"

"I can't wait. Love you, Kel."

She had reached the farm stand anyway.

Abuelo had first opened the stand when his ranch, set on twelve flat acres in the country, started producing more fruits and vegetables than his family could eat on their own.

When Dad took over, he kept the stand open Thursday through Sunday, just like Abuelo, selling produce he had picked the day before.

For as long as Raquel could remember, the farm stand had been a small wooden shed, with handmade shelves and a table where they arranged bushel baskets of green beans or squash or carrots or strawberries—whatever was in season. There wasn't even a cash register, just a metal honor box, where customers dropped folded-up bills or slips of paper with promises to pay next time. It was perfect. It was theirs.

But then Sylvia had burst in, bubbling over with ideas to make the farm stand bigger, more popular. That's how she and Dad met. She worked at the marketing agency Dad hired to help attract new customers.

Last spring, Sylvia convinced him to replace the old shed with a new one, large enough for visitors to browse inside, with space for refrigerated cases filled with new products: cheeses and eggs, and pies from other farms in the area. Dad had worried it wasn't the right time to expand. After all, they were just coming off a statewide lockdown. "We're lucky the business survived," he said.

Then Sylvia nodded, smiled, and opened her laptop. She scrolled through spreadsheets showing the days and times they had the most customers, graphs projecting the money they could earn, news clippings about the farm-to-table movement.

Even Raquel was dazzled.

But now, as Raquel stepped through the entrance and

looked up at a black-and-white picture of the old wooden shed above the new cash register, a homesick knot tightened in her chest. How could it be possible to miss a place when you were standing right in the middle of it?

"Kel! You're a lifesaver. Thanks so much for coming over," Sylvia chirped. Her hair was piled in a loose bun on the top of her head, and she wore a canvas apron over a yellow gingham sundress. "We're swamped, and your dad had to go deal with an irrigation emergency."

Raquel looked around. The harsh August sun was finally softening, and the farm stand buzzed with what Sylvia called the dinner-panic crowd. Panicking because it was almost time to eat, and they didn't know what they were going to make.

"So, what do you need?"

"Tomatoes," Sylvia said, pointing to an overflowing crate. "We're drowning in them. Can you put them in baskets and maybe whip up one of your inspiration boards?"

The boards had been Raquel's idea. Chalkboard signs with recipes and other tips for using the produce.

"Sure thing." She might not be able to come up with a

story, but she had twelve years' worth of ideas for dealing with too many tomatoes.

Raquel overturned one of the buckets that Dad still left around the stand—even though Sylvia complained that they ruined the ambience—and sat down to work.

Sylvia whipped her phone out of her apron pocket and took a picture.

"Hashtag family business," she said, holding up the phone. "Mind if I post it? People love to know who they're buying from."

"Go ahead," Raquel said, examining a San Marzano tomato for bruises. "Family business."

3

Lucinda couldn't help but yawn as she rounded the edge of the apricot orchard the next morning, her footsteps thudding softly on the damp earth. She hoped Jules, who had sped up to jog ahead of her, didn't notice. Even though Lucinda had finally made it a habit to wake up for a run before breakfast, it wasn't what her body wanted to do. Which was sleep. She imagined Crybaby, her soft and lazy tabby, still curled on top of the bed, paw slung over his eyes, and yawned again.

Jules slowed to a stop. "Look, it's Marcos," she said,

pointing. Lucinda caught up and stood next to Jules, hands on her hips while her breathing slowed. Dad was in the middle of a row of apricot trees with Lara, one of the interns from the university's agricultural program. They were pruning. It always made Lucinda a little sad to see the trees look so small and thin afterward. But Dad said pruning made them stronger, that cutting away some growth would let the sunshine in to reach next year's fruit. And they had to do it now to give the trees time to heal before the winter rain.

Lucinda understood. Yet, looking at the pile of branches and leaves left behind, she wondered if it hurt them.

"Good morning!" Jules called out.

Lara waved and moved around to the back of the tree.

Dad rested his clippers against the ladder, wiped his hands on the edge of his flannel shirt, and walked toward them, smiling. "Good morning," he said. "I can't believe you managed to drag her out of bed before noon, Jules. What's your secret?"

Jules laughed.

Lucinda rolled her eyes. "I've been getting up to run

for weeks, Dad." Still, it was true that she and Mom did enjoy sleeping in, especially during the summer. They'd wake up, rubbing their eyes, long after the sun rose to find Raquel already at the kitchen table, writing in her notebook.

"Are you coming in for breakfast?" Jules asked.

"Right after Lara and I get through this row. Why don't you two finish your run, and I'll meet you back there?"

"See you later, then," Jules said, and took off jogging again.

Lucinda started to follow, then stopped. "Don't forget," she said. "You're driving carpool to the rink today."

Dad tapped his temple. "Got it," he said. "Right here on my schedule."

"Oh! Does Kel still make you one?" Kel could be a little annoying with her schedules, the way she tried to manage their lives down to the minute, like they couldn't be trusted to do it themselves. But now that she'd stopped, Lucinda sort of missed finding her sister's overeager notes taped to the refrigerator. *It's Tuesday! Here's the plan!*

Not that she'd ever say so.

"No." Dad shook his head, chuckling. "But maybe I should ask her to. It's a lot of work keeping up with you three."

He picked up his clippers again. Lucinda waved and turned to follow Jules.

Three. It still felt strange to hear, though she wished it didn't. For so long they had been just two. And while Lucinda loved having Jules as a friend, as a training partner—just having her *there*—a small, guilty part of her wondered if she would ever get used to having her as a *sister.*

Her stomach somersaulted with worry, as if Jules could somehow hear her thoughts. She sprinted ahead and finally caught up as Jules was nearing the back of the ranch house.

"I wonder . . . what your mom is . . . making," Lucinda said, slightly breathless. "She's an . . . amazing cook."

They opened the door and stopped just inside to take off their mud-speckled shoes. "You wouldn't say that if you had to live through her experimental phases," Jules replied.

"What's that?" Sylvia called out from the kitchen.

Jules slapped her hand over her mouth. "Nothing," she called back through her fingers.

"We were just saying how much we were looking forward to breakfast," Lucinda covered for her, scooping up Crybaby, who had sauntered to the door to greet them. She glanced back at Jules, and they burst into giggles.

Sylvia eyed them skeptically as they walked into the kitchen, which only made them laugh harder. Lucinda tried to press her lips shut, and her eyes began to water. She buried her face in Crybaby's fur.

"I'm not sure what's so funny," Sylvia said. "But you're right on time. I've been experimenting with some new jams for the wedding, and I want you to test them."

"You first," Jules whispered, nudging Lucinda with her elbow. Lucinda couldn't hold it in anymore. A new stream of giggles burbled out of her. Crybaby meowed in complaint and leaped from her arms.

Sylvia had told them all about her plan to send the wedding guests home with a jar of jam made with fruit from the ranch. One of her colleagues had even designed a special label, with the *M* for Mendoza and the *V* for

Viramontes intertwined in the roots of an oak tree. But she was still looking for the perfect recipe.

Lucinda guessed that Sylvia wanted the fruit to represent the way their families had come together. The way they had blended into something new. It was a nice idea, but Lucinda couldn't help wondering what it meant about the families they had been before.

She didn't want to make Sylvia feel bad, though. Not after everything she and Raquel had put her through, trying to scare her off when they'd first met that spring.

"I'll try it," Lucinda said, stepping forward.

"Thank you, *Lucinda*," Sylvia said. She wiped her hands on the dish towel that was draped over her shoulder and dipped a wooden spoon into the saucepan on the stove. She handed it to Lucinda.

Lucinda blew on the red jam, then slurped a little off the spoon. Sylvia bit her lip, waiting for Lucinda to swallow. Jules folded her arms over her chest and watched, too.

She could taste the strawberry right away. It was light and sweet and reminded her of all the summers she had spent at the ranch. There was a sharper, brighter taste as well. *Lemon*, she thought, *and maybe some mint.* And finally, an unexpected earthiness. She closed her eyes, trying to place it.

"Too much peppercorn, right?" Sylvia asked, grimacing.

"*Pepper?*" Jules asked. "In the *jam?*"

Lucinda opened her eyes. "It's great," she said. "This one's my favorite batch so far."

Sylvia smiled. "Good. Go get cleaned up, and we'll have it over biscuits."

Lucinda licked the rest of the jam off the spoon before dropping it in the sink.

On her way toward the hall, she found Raquel sitting at the table. She was peering at her computer screen and chewing on a handful of Corn Chex. It didn't matter that breakfast was coming up soon. Corn Chex was Raquel's thinking food.

"What are you working on?" Maybe she had finally come up with a story idea. It would be all Raquel would think about or talk about or *care* about until she was finished. But Lucinda could deal with her sister's obsession if it meant an end to the dull fog of boredom she seemed to be walking under for the past few weeks.

"Dresses," Raquel answered with a crunch.

"Huh?" Lucinda stepped closer to the screen. Open on Raquel's lap was one of the wedding magazines Sylvia had brought home. On the computer screen was a spreadsheet with categories listed on top: sleeveless, straps, color, fabric.

Sylvia had asked them to pick out bridesmaids' dresses. But so far it had been impossible to agree on anything.

"Only you would make a chart to pick out a *dress*."

"Well, it's not like those mood boards you and Jules made are going to get us any closer to a decision."

She sounded like herself, like the old bossy Raquel again. Satisfied, Lucinda sniffed and walked toward the bedroom they still shared to change.

4

Anyone come up with
a new story idea?

Alice

Yes! I just started theater camp, and
I came up with something perfect
for you: How will theaters survive
after being shut for a whole year?

Peter

I still think you should write a story
about all the pandemic pets people

33

bought. My grandma just got another cockatiel.

Daisy

Here's one. My cousin Amanda is having a do-over quinceañera. But she'll be turning 16! Can you even call it a quinceañera? Anyway, you should write about all the parties people are having now that we can have parties again. I'll even give you my top five tips!

Lucinda

Why am I still on this group text?! Why is Alice? Aren't you going into high school now? And why are you still bothering the newspaper club, Kel? You're not even the editor!

Sylvia set a mason jar filled with a bunch of marigolds from Abuela's flower garden at the center of the table. Raquel shifted her laptop to make room for it.

Dad had given her the computer earlier that summer, when Sylvia insisted he needed to upgrade the system he was using to manage the farm stand now that it was growing so quickly. It came at the perfect time, since Lu and Raquel had to return the one the school had lent them for distance learning.

To be totally accurate, Dad had given his old laptop to all three girls. But it was Raquel's. They all knew it.

"Don't let me get in your way," Sylvia said, going back to the kitchen. "We still have a few minutes before breakfast. Are you any closer to finding the perfect dress? We should get an order in soon. Sometimes they take a while to ship."

"Four to six weeks," Raquel confirmed, and scooped up another handful of Corn Chex. She had included a column for shipping times in her spreadsheet, too, adding a little extra in case they needed alterations. She and Lu had never dressed alike, even when they were younger. Mom said it was because their personalities were so strong and so different, right from the start. But Raquel suspected it had more to do with the fact that Mom preferred shopping at thrift stores. She loved the savings, and the chance to find something she didn't know she was looking for. She could turn a shopping trip into a treasure hunt.

Sylvia had never asked them to dress alike at the

wedding. But it was almost as if the three of them—Lu and Jules and Kel—had silently agreed that they would. It would be like a team uniform, a way of showing they were in this together.

The dresses were also a distraction. A way for Raquel to keep her mind from running in the same dead-end circles as she struggled to come up with a story idea. But the *Mirror* was never far from her thoughts.

Daisy might be onto something. Maybe Raquel could write about how people were beginning to celebrate again after so many sad and strained months apart. Dad's wedding was the perfect example. But the idea didn't seem quite big enough somehow.

Sylvia had suggested a story about how small businesses like the farm stand had stayed open. "You could interview people all over Lockeford," she'd said. "Georgina's Pies, San Joaquin Creamery . . ."

It wasn't a bad idea, but it also wasn't *hers*.

Sylvia returned from the kitchen balancing a pitcher of orange juice in one arm and a bowl of fruit in the other. "Coming through!"

"Whoa." Raquel sprang from her chair to take the pitcher, right as the juice was about to slosh over the edge.

"Thanks," Sylvia said. "You won't believe this, but I was trying *not* to disturb your work."

"That's all right," Raquel said. "You didn't actually interrupt anything." She could hear Lu and Jules bounding back down the hallway. She wouldn't be able to concentrate much longer anyway. She set down the pitcher, then closed her laptop and carried it to the end table that Sylvia sorted mail on, but that used to be where Abuela kept a picture of their family—Mom, Dad, Lu, and Raquel, that is.

"Hey, Mom!"

"What have I said about yelling across the house, Jules?" Sylvia answered.

Jules and Lu turned the corner into the dining room. "Sorry," Jules said. "But look. The Día de los Muertos 10K is back on!"

She held out her phone. Sylvia took it and squinted at the screen. "They really should have hired us to work on their social media this year," she muttered before handing the phone back to Jules and heading into the kitchen again.

"Not like you would've had any time," Jules said, not quite loud enough for Sylvia to hear. "You're always so busy with the farm stand."

Sylvia came back with a plate full of warm biscuits piled on top of a dish towel. Jules reached for one, but Sylvia swatted her hand away.

She had so many kitchen gadgets—special pans for paella, thermometers for candy, a knife for chopping carrots and a completely different one for peeling apples. But when it came to biscuits, she always rolled out the dough and cut it in circles using the top edge of a regular drinking glass. When Raquel asked why, Sylvia said it was the way her tía Enriqueta taught her.

"You'll let us run, right?" Jules persisted, pulling out her chair. She always chose the seat facing the window, the one Raquel used to think of as Dad's. "Lu says she'll do it with me."

Raquel stiffened. Día de los Muertos was at the beginning of November.

"We'll be home by then," she argued. "Back in LA, I mean."

Lu's hand hovered over a strawberry. Her eyes darted from Raquel to Jules. Raquel could tell she didn't want to let either of them down. "Well . . . I . . . I can always come back for the race, right?"

Jules nodded and sat down, but Raquel kept Lu pinned with her eyes. She didn't like the hint of hesitation in her voice. Like maybe she *wasn't* planning on going home.

"We'll see," Sylvia said, placing one last plate on the table. "You can sign up, but it all depends on whether this virus finally goes away. It's still surging in some parts of the country, you know."

It was why they were planning a small, outdoor wedding at the ranch, with just close family and friends invited.

"We should train," Lu said, taking her place across from Raquel. "I've never run a 10K."

Raquel leaned forward, dates and schedules and color-coded charts already assembling in her mind. "You have, what, about twelve weeks? We can create a training plan. How far you should run each day to work up to it, exercises you can do to build strength. That kind of thing."

Jules reached for the pitcher of orange juice and poured herself a glass. "Oh, you don't have to worry about that," she said. She swallowed a sip before going on. "I already have a plan. Mom and I used to run tons of these races."

Raquel slouched back in her chair.

Lu chewed the edge of her thumbnail. "But Kel can make sure we stay on track," she said. "She's very good with time management."

She looked at Raquel. "You'll help us, right?"

Raquel smiled weakly. "Yeah, sure." But she knew they didn't need it. And Lu's attempt to make her feel useful had the opposite effect.

The screen door rattled as Dad stepped through, stomping the dust off his boots.

Sylvia had taped a bright orange note to the door that said, SHUT ME! Last spring, when they were first getting to know one another, she had accidentally let Crybaby out, and still hadn't quite forgiven herself.

It wasn't *entirely* Sylvia's fault, though. Raquel had noticed that the door wasn't closed and let it happen anyway, hoping to turn her dad and her sister against Sylvia once and for all. Only a few months had passed since then, but it felt like it happened in a completely different lifetime, to a completely different family. Raquel cringed every time she saw that note.

"Perfect timing as usual," Sylvia said when Dad walked into the kitchen. "We just started breakfast." Dad leaned over to kiss her cheek before dropping an armful of zucchini on the counter. Moments like that were so familiar now that Raquel almost didn't notice them anymore. But then she noticed that she hadn't noticed, and was startled all over again that this family she hadn't wanted to begin with had quietly become one anyway.

"I thought I'd make calabacitas tonight," Dad said, turning to wash his hands in the sink.

"Where's Lara?" Jules asked.

"She had to get to class," Dad answered. "You know, you three could learn a lot from her. She's a very good role model." He dried his hands, then reached into his shirt pocket and pulled out a letter. "I ran into Cal, from up the road, just now. He said this letter was delivered to his house by mistake. It's addressed to you, Syl. Looks like it's from Mexico."

Sylvia and Jules jumped out of their chairs. Sylvia took the letter from Dad, and Jules stood at her elbow while she opened it.

"It's from my cousin Elena," Sylvia said. "I'd recognize her handwriting from a mile away."

She pulled a delicate sheet of peach-colored stationery from the envelope and unfolded it. A dried flower fell out and fluttered to the floor. Jules picked it up and held it to her nose.

Lu set her fork down. Raquel swallowed one last bite of biscuit and watched Sylvia's eyes flit over the page. They glistened with excitement at first. Then Sylvia pulled the paper closer and frowned.

"Mi amor?" Dad asked.

Sylvia shook her head. Her shoulders dropped. "She can't come," she murmured. "My tía Enriqueta. She can't come to the wedding."

Jules snatched the letter and started reading, too. Her face fell in exactly the same way Sylvia's had.

Dad draped his arm around Sylvia's shoulders. "¿Qué pasó?"

"Her doctor says it's still too risky to travel," Sylvia said. "I understand. Of course. I would never want to put her in danger. It's just that she practically raised me, and I wanted her to be there to see us . . . To see how far we've come." Tears pooled in the corners of her eyes.

Raquel looked across the table to check on Lu. Her eyes had begun to water, too. She hated to see people cry, especially adults.

"What if we just . . . have the wedding later?" Raquel suggested.

Kel, Lu mouthed.

What? Raquel mouthed back. It seemed like the best solution.

Sylvia dabbed her eyes with a tissue Dad had given her. "Tía Enriqueta would hate to know she caused a delay," she said. "Besides, who knows when things will finally get back to normal?" She pointed at the letter Jules still held tight in her hand. "But Elena says she'll send some obleas, so at least it will *feel* like they're with us."

According to Sylvia, her family in Mexico was famous for their obleas, sweets made with cajeta, a kind of caramel, sandwiched between two thin wafers. She wanted to serve them instead of wedding cake.

"No," Jules said.

Everyone looked at her. Lucinda's eyes widened. Raquel's shoulders tensed.

"I'm disappointed, too, mija," Sylvia said, running a hand through Jules's hair. "But we have to respect—"

"No," Lu repeated, glancing at Raquel, then back at Jules. "She's right. If Tía Enriqueta can't come to the wedding . . ."

Raquel opened her mouth, but for once, she was too late to stop what she now knew was coming.

"Let's bring the wedding to Tía Enriqueta," Jules finished.

5

Dad and Sylvia didn't move. They didn't say a word. They stared at Jules as if trying to figure out if she was serious. Crybaby, lured to the kitchen by the smell of eggs, meowed when he got into the doorway, looked around at all of them, then turned and retreated to his hiding spot underneath the couch in the living room.

Finally, right as Lucinda thought she couldn't stand the silence any longer, Dad broke it. "Why not?"

"*Why not?*" Sylvia echoed. She stepped away from

Dad and looked up into his eyes. "Why not take the wedding to Tía Enriqueta? In *Mexico*?"

Dad grinned. "Yes, in Mexico. Unless she moved somewhere else. And if she did, we'll take the wedding *there*."

The corners of Jules's mouth had begun to turn up into a smile. Lucinda smiled, too, but when she looked at Raquel, she noticed her sister hadn't joined their silent celebration. She was studying Dad's face, as if he was someone she thought she recognized from across a crowded room. Like she couldn't quite place where exactly she knew him from.

Lucinda understood the feeling. If she reached into her memories, back to the time when their parents were still together, she could pull out moments when Dad would take them all by surprise. They would be in the car, heading home from a dinner with cousins, and he'd say, "Should we just keep going? Let's go to San Diego!"

Side by side in the back seat, she and Raquel would cheer. Mom, sitting up front, her hair flying in her face, would laugh. "But we didn't pack anything."

And Dad would squeeze her shoulder and say, "What else do we need?"

But that was a long time ago. And Lucinda couldn't remember the last time Dad even took a vacation. She twisted the edge of her napkin. Maybe Raquel was right not to get swept away with the idea.

"Who are you, and what have you done with my fiancé?" Sylvia teased, turning and stepping toward the table.

Dad caught her fingertips and whirled her back around. "I know how much this means to you," he said. "Let's do it. Let's go to Casas Grandes. The girls are old enough to travel, and it's safer now."

Sylvia shook her head. "We can't."

"Why can't we?" Dad and Jules said together.

Sylvia made her way back to the table. Dad and Jules followed her and sat down.

"Well, for one thing, I don't think you've ever taken a weekend off for as long as I've known you," Sylvia said, serving herself a scoopful of freshly cut fruit and then passing the bowl to Dad. "Our third date involved harvesting cherries."

Dad took the bowl. "That was different. It was cherry season. Anyway, we've hired three more people to run the farm stand. They can look after things while we're gone. Exactly like you said."

Sylvia paused, considering this. "True . . . But do you even have passports?"

"Are you kidding?" Lucinda said, spooning jam onto a warm biscuit. "Like Raquel would *ever* let our passports expire. We all renewed them two years ago. Dad had to come down to LA and everything."

She thought Raquel would at least *appreciate* that Lucinda had remembered. Instead, she was frowning, pushing her eggs around her plate.

Crybaby strolled into the kitchen again and jumped into Lucinda's lap, twitching his tail and begging for a bite. She giggled. "Can Crybaby come, too? I think he should be in the wedding. Can't you see him in a tux?"

Dad shook his head and pointed at the SHUT ME! sign on the door. "I don't think so. We don't want him wandering off in Mexico."

Raquel finally lifted her eyes. "Then what will we do

with him? We can't leave him here by himself. Right, Lu?"

Lucinda held Crybaby against her chest. She hadn't thought about that. And she couldn't drop him off with Mom, either, since she was all the way in New York.

"No problem!" Jules said. "We'll ask one of the other shelter volunteers to take care of him while we're away." She and Sylvia volunteered with the animal shelter. Sylvia made adorable videos to entice people to adopt the pets, and Jules sewed blankets and toys to help them feel a little cozier while they waited to go to their new homes.

"He'll come home so spoiled you won't know what to do with him," Sylvia told Lucinda between sips of orange juice. She set her glass down. "It *would* be nice to be back on Tía Enriqueta's ranch again. It's been so long. You would love it there, Marcos. And you two would have so much in common. You could talk about planting and harvesting, and all that farm stuff."

Dad chuckled. "All that farm stuff?"

Jules sat up straighter. "And we could go horseback riding. And visit the ruins at Paquimé." She grabbed

Lucinda's elbow. "I can show *you two* around for once, and you can meet all my cousins." She paused. "I mean, *our* cousins. Can we go, Mom? Please say yes."

The letter lay forgotten on the counter, as if all the bad news it delivered had blown away in the gust of Jules's excitement.

"Well?" Dad asked. He took Sylvia's hand and squeezed.

She blinked hard, as if she still couldn't believe what was happening. "Well . . . how can I argue with all of you? I guess we're planning a destination wedding!"

Jules leaped from her chair, scaring Crybaby, who skittered back to the couch. "You guys are going to *love* it in Casas Grandes."

Raquel still hadn't said anything. Lucinda thought she would have jumped at the chance to travel, to see more of the world, to get out of Lockeford and find new stories.

"Wait!" Raquel said. Her eyes met Lucinda's, and she dropped her voice as if she was talking to her sister alone. As if they were four-year-olds again, under their covers and whispering in the dark. "I don't think this is a good idea."

"But why?" Lucinda whispered back.

"I . . . don't know . . . what about . . . what about," Raquel sputtered. "The synchronized skating team! You're always saying how important it is to do things together, and now you're going to abandon your teammates for some getaway?"

Lucinda laughed, mostly relieved. It was nice of Raquel to think about the team, but she didn't have to worry.

"It's not just *some getaway*. It's Dad's wedding. They'll understand."

"Especially if you bring them souvenirs," Jules added. "We can show you all the shops."

But Raquel wasn't satisfied.

"What about school? It's starting soon. We can't drop everything and fly off to Mexico!"

"That's true, Marcos," Sylvia said.

"Well then," Dad said, shoveling one last forkful of fruit into his mouth. "What are you all waiting for? We better start packing!"

Raquel pushed her chair away from the table, stood, and stomped out the back door, letting it clatter behind her.

6

Raquel hadn't thought about where she would go. She just started walking. Across the patio where Jules had left the dye-tinged bucket, then past the vegetable garden that was still overflowing with tomatoes. Out of habit, she pulled her phone from her pocket to check the *Manzanita Mirror*. It wasn't as if she was *hoping* the site would have crashed since the last time she looked. Or that she'd find a typo big enough that she'd have to point it out to Ms. King. She only wanted some evidence that the *Mirror* still needed her.

Instead, what she saw when the page loaded was that Paul had updated the top story yet again. It was the second time in the past twenty-four hours. Why was that allowed? How was it even possible? She only updated once a week when she was in charge.

Raquel stopped at one of the wind-twisted oak trees near the barn. She wasn't as good at climbing as Lu. She wasn't as strong or as flexible or, if she was being *totally* honest, as fearless. She liked having her feet on the ground, thank you. But this tree had a low, sturdy branch, as if it had knelt down on purpose to make things easier for her. And because of that, she had always thought of it as hers. She put her phone back in her pocket, planted her leg on the branch, and pulled herself up.

Already, she was beginning to feel bad about storming off. Maybe she should have stayed in the kitchen to talk about it. But her thoughts were so jumbled, she needed a minute alone to sort them out and put them back in order again. Raquel closed her eyes, leaned against the rough bark, and tried to figure out why she didn't want to go to Mexico and, more importantly, what she could do about it.

But before she could settle in, she heard the rhythmic thud of footsteps coming toward her.

She didn't turn around. She focused on the footsteps, trying to guess who it was. Not Jules. If it had been Jules, the steps would have been faster. Jules ran everywhere. It was strange to have someone in the house whose feet raced as fast as Raquel's thoughts. No wonder it felt like they were crashing into each other sometimes.

It couldn't have been Sylvia, either. These footsteps were steady and sure. Sylvia's would have been lighter, more cautious. She said she loved the ranch, but she didn't know its every corner the way the rest of them did. She worried about tripping over gopher holes or snagging her shirt on a wild raspberry bush. She also would have wanted to give Raquel some space.

It definitely wasn't Lu. As soon as she was in shouting distance, Lu would have been trying to fix things, to calm her down, to beg her not to make a big deal out of this even though they both knew it was, in fact, a very big deal.

There was only one other person it could be. Raquel looked back.

"Hey, Dad."

He closed the space between them in three strides and stood at the base of the tree, looking up. He put his hands on his hips, gauged the distance from the ground to the limb Raquel was sitting on, then asked, "Is there room for one more up there?"

Raquel had expected him to tell her to come down. To scold her for leaving in a huff.

She had *not* expected this.

"Seriously?"

"What, you think I can't make it up there?"

Raquel inched over on the branch to give him room. "I don't know, but I'd love to see you try." It was true. She would. He hadn't climbed trees with them since they were little, running around the ranch with their cousins in the summer. He'd chase them up trees sometimes or hide in the branches to jump down and startle Mom.

Now Dad rolled up his sleeves and stretched his arms in an exaggerated warm-up. Like a cartoon version of Lu, which made Raquel laugh despite how unsettled she still was. He grabbed hold of the lowest branch and jammed his foot into the crevice where it met the trunk. As he pulled himself up, his foot slipped and he began to slide down. Raquel gasped and reached out, even though there was no way she could have lifted him up on her own. But he caught himself, and soon he was sitting on the branch beside her.

"See?" he said, taking off his baseball hat to smooth his hair, then putting it back on again. "I still have it in me." But even he seemed slightly surprised that he'd actually managed it.

Raquel swung her legs, listening to the birds chirping and to the far-off sound of a tractor. She wished Dad would get it over with and *say* whatever it was he had come out here to say, instead of making her speak first. But he didn't.

"I know I shouldn't have stormed off," Raquel said, giving in. "I'm sorry." She looked at Dad, wondering if it was enough. Still, he was silent. It was a reporter's trick—stay quiet and let the other person squirm until they tell you more than they meant to. She couldn't believe she was falling for it, but she also couldn't help it.

"I just . . . I don't know . . . I guess I felt like no one cared what *I* thought."

Dad stared at her. "What *you* thought? About Sylvia and me getting married? We talked to the three of you, and you said you were all right with it, but if you're not—"

Raquel held up her hand to stop him.

"No, it's not that. I told you, I *am* all right with you getting married." She wondered if anyone would ever believe her. The plan to get Mom and Dad back together, to scare off Sylvia? Lu had gone along with it for a while, but it had all been Raquel's idea. And no matter how much time had gone by, no matter how many long, honest talks they had, Raquel wasn't sure they would ever forget it.

"Then what?" Dad asked.

Raquel looked away. It seemed small now, especially compared to a wedding. Especially after Lu had given up skating with her team. "It's . . ." she started to say, then changed her mind. "It's . . . nothing."

"I didn't climb *all* the way up here for nothing."

Raquel glanced down and smiled. The branch didn't even come up to Dad's head. They weren't very high at all.

"Fine," she said, and took a deep breath. "It's that since we've been up here, I had to give up editing the school newspaper for the summer, and now some new kid is in charge, and he's doing such a great job that I'm worried Ms. King is going to make *him* the editor next year instead of me, and I can't do anything about it, and if we go to Mexico, I'll be even *farther* away."

The confession left her breathless, but also lighter. She looked at Dad to see if he was angry, if he thought she was being selfish or silly.

Instead, he nodded.

"You've given up a lot over the past few months. All of you have." He was quiet for a moment. "I'll talk to Sylvia. You're an important part of this family. We want you to be part of the ceremony, but more than anything, we want you to be happy."

It felt like when a teacher announces she's giving everyone an extra day to prepare for a big test. A rush of relief that makes you realize how much you were dreading the thing you thought was coming.

"So I don't have to go with you?" Raquel asked,

double-checking what she thought he was saying.

"It would mean a lot to me to have you there," he answered. "And it would mean a lot to Sylvia. But the choice is yours. I won't force you to come. Maybe we can postpone after all. Until everything is back to normal."

It would have been easier if he had told her she *had* to go to Mexico, Raquel realized. She couldn't ask them to postpone the wedding for her. Who knew when anything would be "normal" again or what that even meant anymore? Even if Dad said the decision was hers, his voice—tender and serious—couldn't disguise what he hoped the decision would be.

Leaves crunched on the ground below them. Raquel looked down again. Lu stood at the bottom of the tree, loose curls shaken out of her bun.

"Of *course* you're coming."

7

The words that had just come out of Dad's mouth were even more shocking than the fact that he was sitting in a tree. Which was saying something. Lucinda waited for him to settle this misunderstanding—which was *obviously* what it was—the way he used to when they were younger. He'd get Raquel to back down from one of her stubborn opinions and convince Lucinda to take a deep breath before her worries spun out of control. He'd help them find their way to the compromise that had been there all along, hiding in plain sight like the letters in a word search.

She said it again, to herself this time: *Of course she's coming*. This was Dad and Sylvia's wedding, the first moments they'd officially be a family. If they weren't all together, would it even count?

When Dad didn't respond, Lucinda assumed he hadn't heard her. She stepped closer to the tree. "You don't mean that, right?" she asked. "You're going to make her come with us? To *Mexico*?" she added, in case it wasn't clear. Right at that moment, she couldn't be sure of anything.

She widened her eyes at Raquel, sending a silent question up through the tree trunk. *What is going on?*

Raquel didn't answer. She shifted on the branch and let her eyes land somewhere over Lucinda's head.

Dad jumped from the tree in one smooth movement. "I'll let the two of you talk," he said. "Bring some corn to the farm stand on your way back? Sylvia says we're running low."

And just like that, without solving anything—without even *trying*—Dad walked back to the house. Lucinda leaned against the tree trunk. Raquel wasn't going to be able to get down without getting past her.

She bit the edge of her thumbnail and wished she could figure out what her sister was up to. She had been acting strange lately, and now Lucinda understood why. Raquel was trying to sabotage the wedding.

"You can go on ahead to the vegetable garden," Raquel said. "I'll catch up."

"Nice try," Lucinda answered. "I'm not moving until you come down."

Raquel groaned. She scooted toward the trunk and stretched her leg toward the ground, trying to jump the way Dad had. But her toes didn't reach, and she slid back onto the branch.

"Come on," Lucinda said. "It's not that high. Just jump."

Raquel shook her head. "I'll climb down the way I came up." She inched backward, looking over her shoulder, hands clinging tight to the branch.

This was going to take all day.

"Grab my hands," Lucinda said, stretching her arms up.

Raquel stopped and looked down at her doubtfully. "You can't catch me. You're not strong enough."

"I'm stronger than you think," Lucinda said. She wiggled her fingers. "Just grab my hands."

Raquel reached with one arm. The other still clung to the tree.

"Come on," Lucinda told her again, more gently as she realized her sister was actually scared and not just hardheaded. It was the same reason she put up with Raquel's bossiness so often. "You can let go."

Finally, Raquel let Lucinda take her other hand. She squeezed her eyes shut and pushed herself off the branch, letting out a choked scream as she came down, bracing her weight on Lucinda. Both of them tumbled to the ground, laughing. And for a moment, Lucinda forgot about Mexico, forgot about Mom and Dad. It was just the two of them again.

But the moment passed as quickly as it had come. Their laughter trailed away.

"Guess we should go get that corn," Raquel said, standing and dusting off her shorts. They walked toward the garden that Abuelo had planted, that they had helped care for every summer for as long as Lucinda could remember. She gnawed on her nail again, still wondering what Raquel was plotting. She wasn't going to get pulled into another one of those schemes. Not after they had come so far.

"It's not going to work, you know," she forced herself to say when they got to the rows of cornstalks.

Raquel flicked an ant off her shoulder. "What's not going to work?"

Lucinda stomped her foot. "Your . . . plan. This . . . whatever it is," she said. "Whatever you're trying to do by refusing to come to Mexico with us, it's not going to work." Even if she didn't know exactly what it was yet, she knew there had to be a plan. With Raquel, there was always a plan. "Dad and Sylvia are getting married. We can't stop it. I don't *want* to stop it."

Raquel grabbed the tangled ends of her brown hair and tugged. "For the last time, I am *not* trying to stop the wedding! Why won't anyone believe me?" She paused, took a deep breath in through her nose, and blew out through her mouth. It was an exercise Lucinda had learned from her new skating coach, Sunny, then taught to Raquel. She was impressed Raquel had remembered.

"I just don't want to go to Mexico," Raquel continued, her voice more even this time. "And I don't want to be in Lockeford anymore. I don't have anything to *do* here. I want to go home."

Lucinda dropped six green ears of corn into one of the plastic crates that were always scattered around the garden. The corn fell to the bottom with a quiet thud. She wanted to say, *This* is *home*. But she understood what Raquel meant, and she felt like all that corn had just landed in her stomach. She was so busy having an amazing summer that it had been easy to ignore the fact that Kel . . . wasn't.

Maybe she should let Raquel have her way, get back to the newspaper and back to Los Angeles. "But I can't go to Mexico by myself," she said, not sure whether she was arguing with herself or with her sister.

"You won't be by yourself," Raquel replied, twisting an ear of corn off its stalk.

"You know what I mean," Lucinda said.

Raquel nodded. She knew.

"You'll have Jules."

Lucinda considered this. "Yeah," she said, giving the ear she was holding a sharp tug. "But all her cousins will be there, too, and I'll be the only one who doesn't speak Spanish."

Raquel turned to face her. "You could practice," she said. "I could set up a schedule. They have all those courses online, and maybe Mom could tutor you on video chat." Raquel's eyes brightened in the way they always did when a new plan began to take shape behind them. When she was getting ready to take charge of a situation.

Progress, Lucinda thought.

In her excitement, Raquel dropped one of the ears she was holding. It fell and rolled in the dirt. She bent to pick it up, then tossed it on top of the pile in the crate. "You'd have to give up even more time with your skating team, but you could probably make a lot of progress if you started right away."

She'd said *you*. Not *we*. Once Raquel had made up her mind about something, it felt nearly impossible to change it. Like trying to uproot one of the ranch's giant oak trees with her bare hands.

"Kel, please," Lucinda begged. "It won't be the same without you. You *have* to come. I'll do anything."

Raquel stepped out from behind a cornstalk. *"Anything?"*

Lucinda gulped. She had no idea what Raquel had in mind. But whatever it was, it had to be better than going to Mexico without her sister. "Anything," she agreed. She lowered her voice. "Seriously, Kel. I can't do this without you. I *need* you there. Just say you'll come."

Raquel looked out over the vegetable garden, then straight at Lucinda.

"If it means that much to you, I'll *think* about it," Raquel said. "But if I decide to go, you owe me. Once we get *home*. To *Los Angeles*."

8

Raquel tapped on her phone to read Mom's last text message one more time.

Mom

> You'll be fine, mi amor. Try to have some fun. Soak it all in the way you always do. And don't forget to send me a postcard! I'll see you soon.

She fought the urge to click over to the *Manzanita Mirror* site to see whether Paul had updated the front page again. In the whirl of packing and planning and searching for airplane tickets over the past week, there hadn't been time to think about it. Raquel had felt almost at home again, settling into the familiar routine of making lists and double-checking that they were all on schedule.

Jules had joined Lu and Raquel in the little apartment over the barn for hours after dinner every night, helping them brush up their Spanish. It was the most time they'd spent together, all three of them, maybe ever. Twice they fell asleep up there in a giggling heap.

But now, in the back seat of a station wagon driven by Elena's husband, Luis, Raquel couldn't help wondering what was happening back home. She couldn't help wishing she was there. She reminded herself of the promise Lu had made. She had agreed to do "anything" if Raquel came along. "Anything" had to include returning to Los Angeles when summer was over, didn't it? That made the whole trip worth it.

Raquel took her plastic cup from the cup holder and sipped a little of the juice Dad had bought them from a converted bus parked on the highway an hour or so outside Chihuahua City. Then she pressed her forehead against the window and looked out. As Jules and Lu dozed next to her, she snapped a picture of puffy white clouds hanging low over a field where horses grazed. It didn't look so different from Lockeford, really, she decided, peering at the phone screen.

Stories were everywhere, she reminded herself. You just had to watch out for them. And maybe if she wrote something here in Mexico, Ms. King would be impressed.

On second thought, Paul would probably get to edit it. She wouldn't be able to bear that. Raquel dropped her phone in her lap.

Suddenly, Jules sat up in the middle seat and rubbed her eyes. Then she grabbed both Lu and Raquel by their shoulders and shook them. "We're almost there!" she said, as if something in the air had changed.

"What? Huh?" Lu mumbled groggily. "Just a few more minutes, okay?" They'd left Lockeford before dawn to make it to the airport on time. And after almost eight hours on two flights, followed by three more hours on the road to the Viramontes family home outside Casas Grandes, everyone was tired.

But the news that they had nearly made it sent a jolt of energy through Raquel. "How do you know?" she asked, leaning over Jules to get a look through the front windshield.

Jules shrugged. "I can feel it."

In the front seat, Sylvia pointed to a spot on the horizon, directing Dad's eyes to a narrow dirt road that curled off the highway. "We're home," she whispered.

Minutes later, Luis steered the station wagon through an iron gate that had been left open for them. At the end of the road was a house with pink stucco walls that stretched wide across the grassy landscape. The sun had begun to set behind the mountains in the distance.

Sylvia said it used to be a working ranch—not like Rancho Los Robles, which was smaller and didn't have any animals. Her grandparents used to raise goats here and planted rows of apple trees. Most of the goats were gone, and they didn't farm much anymore. But the family still kept horses and rented the ranch's many rooms to travelers who came for the pottery workshops and to explore the nearby ruins.

They called the ranch Flor de Manzana, or apple blossom. Sylvia had been worried that Elena would have to cancel reservations in order to hold a last-minute wedding there. But it turned out there weren't any. People were still getting sick, and business was still slow.

Sylvia and Jules had talked so much about the ranch over the past few days—its rose garden with the fountain in the middle and its red-tile roof—that their memories had blurred into Raquel's. Like watercolor paints that seep past their borders. She felt like she almost recognized the place.

Luis slowed and parked. Jules unbuckled her seat belt before he even turned off the engine.

The heavy wooden front door, with violet bougainvillea creeping up the walls on either side, flew open. A woman, two girls, and a boy came running down the stone walkway. A dog with shaggy black hair scrambled after them, tail wagging.

"Elena!" Sylvia yelled, waving at the woman, who had the same red-brown hair as Jules. She tugged Dad's arm. "¡Vamos!"

Dad laughed as he fiddled with the door lock. "I'm going!" When he finally opened it, Sylvia practically pushed him out in her rush.

Jules didn't wait for Lu or Raquel to open their doors. She clambered over Raquel's lap and tumbled out of the car before Raquel even registered what was happening.

"Sarita!" she shouted. "Alejandra! Mateo!" The dog barreled toward her and jumped, resting his paws on her shoulders. Jules laughed as he licked her cheek. "Oso! I missed you, too, buddy!" Then she turned back to Lu and Raquel. "Come on!"

Raquel knew their faces from photos in the scrapbooks Sylvia had opened on the coffee table while they prepared for the trip. Flipping through the pages, Raquel had realized that she never thought about Jules and Sylvia having their own family, their own memories and traditions. As if, in her imagination, their story began when it collided into hers. But now here they all were, right in the middle of it.

Sylvia, nose pink from happy crying, pulled Dad and Lu and Raquel into the crush of cousins.

She looped her arm through Dad's. "This is him, this is Marcos," she said in Spanish. Elena threw her arms around Dad's neck. He stumbled backward with the force of it. Then Elena let go and stood in front of Lu and Raquel. She took one of them under each arm and hugged them, too. "Mucho gusto," Lu whispered in her website Spanish. Elena squeezed even tighter.

Sylvia looked over their heads, into the house. "Where's Tía Enriqueta? Does she know we're here?"

Elena loosened her hold on Raquel's shoulder.

"She . . . she is so happy to see you again, but . . . she's . . . had a long day, and she's gone to lie down," Elena explained. Even though she was speaking Spanish, Raquel could tell she was grasping for words. She changed the subject. "You all must be tired, too. And hungry. Come in, come in."

Sylvia frowned. "Gone to lie down?" she repeated, as if trying to make sense of it. Raquel didn't understand, either. Wasn't Tía Enriqueta the reason they had come?

Then Sylvia sighed and led Dad into the tiled entryway. Sarita and Alejandra, pulling Jules by the wrist, darted after them, with Mateo and Oso close behind.

"Should we go with them?" Lu asked.

"What about our bags?"

Jules called back, "We'll get them later. Right now I want to show you *everything*!"

Lu smiled and hurried ahead, leaving Raquel on her own.

"I'll be right there," she said, though she was pretty sure no one was listening anymore.

She found her duffel in the station wagon, unzipped it, and pulled out a fresh notebook and pen. If there happened to be a story lurking around this house, she didn't want to miss it. She stuck the pen behind her ear and shoved the notebook in her pocket, then made her way to the door.

She followed Jules's voice down a long hallway whose walls were lined with black-and-white pictures of the family. She stopped to look at one of the photos because she thought, at first, it was of Jules. It wasn't, though. It was another girl who looked a lot like her, holding a baby goat in her arms.

"Kel! In here!"

Raquel spun around and saw Lucinda waving from inside a bedroom. She and Jules were stretched across a window seat overlooking the rose garden and a gnarled old olive tree that grew at the center of it.

"Isn't it the most beautiful place you ever saw?" Lu asked.

Before Raquel could argue, Jules sprang from the window seat. "The best part is there are secret passages left over from the Mexican Revolution. These closets are connected!" She flung open the closet door and pushed aside some spare blankets to reveal a narrow crawlspace. "It leads straight through—"

"To my room?" Raquel asked, peeking inside. She and Lu had always wanted a secret passageway, and Mom always asked, "What for?" since they were never very far apart.

Jules, still crouched inside the closet, bit her lower lip and looked from Lu to Raquel. "To mine," she said. "But yours is just a few doors down, Kel. Me and Mom thought you'd love the old study."

9

Hey, Mom, we made it to Mexico! Kel says we'll probably be home before this gets to you, but I'm sending it anyway because I know you love getting postcards. And also because I want to say I wish you were here, except that'd be weird. But on a postcard, it's a normal thing to say, right? Wish you were here. Love, Lucinda.

Lucinda meant to tell Raquel that she should bring the blanket and pillow from the study to sleep on the floor in her room. Or that they could both squeeze onto the twin bed the way they did when they stayed with Tía Regina, Mom's sister, for the weekend. But then she'd been so tired from their long day of travel that, after eating a few sips of the garlic soup Elena served, she'd collapsed on the bed and hadn't woken up until sunshine was pouring through the window.

She stretched, realizing it was the first time a bedroom had been hers alone before. Those times she and Raquel, annoyed and needing space from each other, had divided their room with clothesline and a bedsheet didn't count.

Someone left her suitcase next to a dresser with bright roses—red, purple, and turquoise—painted on its drawers. On the opposite wall, near the closet, was a writing desk and a chair with a wool blanket draped over it.

Lucinda flung her legs off the edge of the bed. All that was missing was Crybaby. He would have leaped onto the window seat and found a patch of sunlight to nap in. "Maybe next time," she said to herself.

But the stillness didn't last. A moment later, there was a knock on the door. It was if her sister could sense she was awake. "Hey, Kel," she said.

The door creaked open.

"It's me." Jules poked her head in. "I was going to use the secret passageway, but I wasn't sure you were up yet, and I didn't want to scare you. Can I come in?"

Lucinda yawned and waved her through.

In one hand, Jules was carrying a plate with a tortilla, some scrambled eggs, and a small, round cookie on it. In the other, she held a clay mug.

"It's Elena's special hot chocolate," she said, setting the mug on the desk. She held the plate out to Lucinda.

Lucinda's stomach growled. She hadn't eaten a full meal since Lockeford. "You're my hero," she said, reaching for the plate.

Even though Coach Sunny would definitely not approve of sweets this early, Lu went for the cookie—two paper-thin wafers with a dollop of caramel sandwiched between them. They were on vacation, weren't they? The wafers broke apart easily between her teeth, and the creamy caramel filling oozed out the sides.

"Okay, this?" Lu said, wiping a crumb from the corner of her mouth. "Is amazing."

"I know." Jules pulled out the desk chair and sat down. "That's an oblea. Mom and Elena say it's more like candy than a cookie. They never let us eat them before breakfast. I had to sneak one out for you."

"An oblea?" Lu asked. "This is what your mom's been talking about?" She was beginning to understand why Sylvia wanted so badly to serve them at the wedding.

"The filling is cajeta, made from goat's milk," Jules said. "My great-great-grandparents brought the recipe up with them from Guanajuato and sold it to a big candy company. But Tía Enriqueta says their version doesn't even come *close* to the original. It's missing a secret ingredient."

Jules picked at a loose fiber on the blanket, stood to look out the window, then sat down again. She suddenly reminded Lucinda of Crybaby, a ball of nervous energy.

"Do you know where my sister is . . . I mean *our* . . . I mean . . ." Lu stopped, reached for the hot chocolate, and took a sip. "I mean, where's Raquel?"

"She and your dad got up super early," Jules answered, straightening the stack of stationery left on the desk for the guests who usually stayed at Flor de Manzana. "Mom says they went out to explore the ranch. We can go look for them, or . . ."

Lucinda tore off a piece of tortilla and used it to scoop up some scrambled egg. "Or?"

"Or . . . Sarita and Alejandra are going to the market to buy a few things that Elena forgot," Jules continued. "We can go with them, but you'd have to hurry up and get ready."

Lucinda set the plate on her lap and twisted a strand of hair around her finger. "Maybe we should wait for Dad and Kel to get back," she said. "Kel would want to see the market, too." Lucinda could imagine her, notebook in hand. Maybe she'd even find that story she was looking for.

Jules crossed the room and plopped down on the bed. "No time," she said. "If we get to the market too late, all the good stuff will be gone, and Mom wants the tardeada to be perfect."

"Tardeada?"

"A little party, later this afternoon," Jules explained "Everyone is coming to meet you—the rest of our cousins, some neighbors—"

Lucinda cringed. *More* people? She had been nervous

enough about meeting the ones who lived at the ranch.

"Don't worry," Jules said. "They'll love you. And we can show Kel the market some other time."

As long as Kel would get another chance . . . "All right, I'm in!" Lucinda said, devouring another mouthful of egg. "Give me five minutes."

Sarita and Alejandra raced from stall to stall, buying tomatillos from one and guavas from another. Lucinda strained to pick out familiar words in their bursts of conversation with the vendors.

"It's usually so much busier," Jules said, looking around as they strolled through the market. "I bet the tourists will start coming back soon."

"They better," Alejandra said, returning with the bag of dried hibiscus flowers Sylvia had requested. She was going to use them to make agua de jamaica to serve at the tardeada. "We need the business."

The shopping finished, they all walked back to the ranch, dropping off a postcard for Mom on the way.

At the house, Sylvia stood in the kitchen at the center of a flurry of chopping and stirring and wiping and sweeping.

She saw them and beamed.

"Oh good!" she said. "You found the jamaica!" She started to walk toward them, but then Oso bolted in front of her, his nails clicking on the tile floor. Sylvia groaned. "¡Oso! ¡Afuera!"

"That's okay," Jules said, laughing as Sylvia chased Oso out of the kitchen. "I know what to do."

Lucinda scanned the room for Raquel and found her sitting at a round table, sorting dried pinto beans with two boys—more cousins, probably. They were so small that they had to sit with their legs folded underneath them to reach.

"There you are. Jules and I are going to make a drink for the party. Want to help?"

Raquel looked up. "I don't know," she said in English, winking at the boys. "This is a very important job. Can the two of you handle it without me?"

They giggled. Raquel stood and followed Lucinda over to Jules, who was waiting with a pitcher in front of the last bit of empty counter space.

She wore an apron and tossed two more at Lucinda and Raquel. It felt strangely like another one of Jules's crafts, Lucinda thought as she tied the strings around her neck.

"The flowers can stain," Jules explained. She filled a pot with water, and Lucinda and Raquel emptied the bag of flowers into it.

"Now it needs to boil." Jules carried the pot to the stove, and as the water slowly warmed, it began to turn a deep, dark red.

"Wait a minute, this is another one of your tie-dye projects, isn't it?" Raquel asked, taking a picture with her camera.

"No, but you just gave me a really good idea," Jules answered, grinning.

Lucinda felt a rush of warmth and sweetness that wasn't from the bubbling liquid. It was that this noisy kitchen, filled with people—and one large dog—she had just met, felt a tiny bit like home.

After a while, all the flowers sank to the bottom. "That's how you know it's ready," Jules said. "Now we have to strain it."

They turned off the burner. Lucinda and Raquel held either side of the pot and carefully emptied it into a glass jar that Jules was holding. A mesh cloth stretched over the top caught the flowers so that all that was left in the jar was red syrup.

When they were done pouring, Jules ladled some of the syrup into a pitcher. "We'll save the rest for later," she said, tightening a lid on the jar. Next, she filled the pitcher with water, and when that was done, said, "All that's left is a cup of sugar."

"Too much, Julieta!" Sylvia called over her shoulder. "*Half* a cup."

"Half a cup and a little extra," Jules whispered.

Raquel smiled. "I'll get it." She took a clay bowl from the counter. It had a scoop inside, and she was about to pour some into the pitcher when Sylvia caught her wrist.

Raquel looked up, confused.

"Mija," Sylvia said, "that's the salt."

"Oh. Sorry," Raquel said, her cheeks turning red as she emptied the granules back into the bowl. Sylvia's family chuckled softly behind her.

Sylvia ruffled Raquel's hair and passed her a different jar. "Try this one," she said with a wink.

Then, as Raquel was scooping up a half cup of sugar, Jules said, "At least it was an *accident* this time." She laughed to herself.

Raquel dropped the scoop back in the jar. Lucinda winced, hoping no one else had heard.

"*Jules,*" Lucinda said under her breath. "Don't."

But it was too late.

"Accident?" asked Sarita, who had taken over Raquel's spot, sorting beans. "What do you mean?"

"I didn't tell you?" Jules said, raising her voice so it would reach across the kitchen. "Last spring, when Kel and Lu first came to Lockeford, Kel was trying to get rid of us, and she played this prank where she sprinkled garlic powder all over one of Mom's cakes. It was disgusting!" She laughed even harder.

And suddenly, the kitchen that had felt like home a minute ago didn't belong to them anymore. Lucinda took the sugar bowl from Raquel's hands, scooped some into the pitcher, and silently stirred.

10

Raquel stared at the pitcher of agua de jamaica, glowing red on the table in the late-afternoon sun. The garlic incident—along with all the other things she had done to push Sylvia away—felt like it had happened so long ago. It was easy to let herself believe that maybe it hadn't happened at all, or at least that no one remembered. That's what Sylvia had told her, wasn't it? *We'll just forget this ever happened.*

But it wasn't so long ago really, and obviously Jules hadn't forgotten. Maybe she never would.

"Would you like me to pour you some?" One of Sylvia's cousins asked Raquel in Spanish, pointing at the pitcher. At least none of the friends and relatives gathered at the long banquet table seemed to hold it against her. Maybe they hadn't even been paying attention.

"Oh," Raquel said. "Sí." The woman filled Raquel's glass with the jamaica—sweetened with sugar, not salt—and dropped a sprig of mint on top.

Raquel thanked her, then looked across the table at Lu, who had her cell phone out. Raquel could tell without seeing the screen that Lu was flipping through pictures of Crybaby, showing them to Alejandra, who leaned over her to see.

"Look at this one! He just loves to nap in that corner of the closet for some reason." Lu sighed at the image as if she were seeing it for the first time. Her finger swiped across the screen, and she squealed.

"And here he is in the laundry basket! He made a nest with all those towels. We had to wash them again, but it was worth it."

Alejandra reached for the phone for a better look.

"What's his name?"

"Hmm." Lu thought about it. "We call him Crybaby. It's like . . ." She paused, searching for the right word.

"¡Chillón!" Jules shouted from her chair next to Alejandra.

Through her giggles, Alejandra protested, "But he's so cute!"

"You wouldn't say that if you had to hear him whine all day," Raquel grumbled. But she wasn't really complaining. Crybaby had grown on her, and even if she wouldn't admit it to Lu, she missed him, too.

"Stop!" Lu said, kicking her under the table. "He doesn't whine. He just . . . voices his opinion. And it's *adorable*. Look at this one." She took the phone back and flipped to a new picture.

Alejandra clapped her hand over her mouth, like the sight of Crybaby was more cuteness than she could handle. "Amá," she said, turning to the far end of the table. "Can we get a gato?"

"We have more animals than we can take care of around here as it is," Elena answered.

"I still don't think it's fair that Oso wasn't invited to the party." Sarita sniffed.

"Don't worry," Jules whispered. "We'll make sure he comes to the wedding."

Elena shot them a warning glance, then went back to her conversation.

Mateo, who sat next to Raquel, swallowed the bite of jicama he had been chewing.

"Maybe after dinner we can take you to see the goats," he suggested.

Sarita nodded. Her dark bangs fell into her eyes. "¡Son preciosas!"

Jules reached over Alejandra and grabbed Lu's wrist. "Yes! You have to see the goats," she said. "You're going to love them."

Lu's eyes darted across the table. "That sounds fun, right?" she asked Raquel. But what she meant was *You'll come, too?*

"Sure," Raquel said, uncertain whether Lu really wanted her there or whether she was just trying to smooth things over again. Raquel reached to the center of the table and took one of the bolillos that was piled on a blue ceramic tray. She checked to make sure none of the adults were watching, then pulled off a chunk of bread and popped it in her mouth.

Dad and Sylvia were at the other end of the table. Dad laughed and talked as if he had always belonged there. As if he had known Sylvia's family for years instead of barely twenty-four hours.

Next to him, at the head of the table, was an empty seat. Raquel guessed it was saved for Tía Enriqueta. No one had said so, but Raquel also guessed that the reason they weren't eating yet was that Tía Enriqueta hadn't joined them.

She was surprised they still hadn't met her. When Sylvia tried to introduce them this morning, Elena said she'd already left. That she had an important meeting about something to do with horses. Raquel had strained to understand Elena's explanation but couldn't translate fast enough.

Yet, of all the people in Sylvia's family, it was Tía Enriqueta whom Raquel felt like she knew best. Partly, that was because of all the stories Sylvia and Jules had been telling. About how Tía Enriqueta was tough— "batalladora," Sylvia had called her—but also curious. About how she was the only one who knew the original candy recipe that had made the family famous.

But Raquel had also gotten to know Tía Enriqueta through the books in the study.

She'd had trouble falling asleep the night before. The room felt too still, the noises outside too different from what she was used to. The moonlight reflected too brightly in the tall, narrow mirror that hung, looking oddly out of place, on one wall. And, of course, she didn't have Lu in a bunk below her.

Shelves filled with dark and dusty books took up most of the room. Raquel had run her finger along their spines until she came to one whose familiar blue cover, with its silhouette of a girl detective, stopped her. It was part of a series, lined up, one through ten, in a neat row. Abuela had a set just like it stored away in the apartment above the barn back in Lockeford. Though hers were in English.

Raquel took down the first book and opened its cover.

Written in graceful but firm cursive in the top corner was a name: *Keta*. It must have been short for Enriqueta the way Kel was short for Raquel. And at the center of the page, fastened with yellowing tape, was a list of names and dates organized into two columns: *Prestado* and *Devuelto*.

"Borrowed and returned," Raquel had murmured.

By the next afternoon at the tardeada, when Tía Enriqueta finally stepped through the arched entryway and onto the patio, she looked exactly the way Raquel had imagined her. She had Juliette's reddish-brown hair— only a little lighter and with streaks of silver at the temples—and the same serious but glimmering eyes of the girl in the black-and-white photo Raquel had seen in the hallway.

The table, crackling with laughter and conversation a moment earlier, settled as she made her way to the empty chair.

"Tía!" Sylvia exclaimed, eyes already filling with tears as she stood to hug her aunt. Dad stood, too, and Jules rushed toward them, dropping her napkin as she jumped from her seat. It was almost an exact reenactment of that moment back in Lockeford, when Sylvia learned that Tía Enriqueta wouldn't be able to make the trip to the wedding. Only this time, Sylvia was crying with joy instead of disappointment. Raquel looked across the table at Lu, who was capturing the reunion on her phone.

She tapped the screen to stop the video, then raised her eyebrows like question marks to Raquel. Were they supposed to greet Tía Enriqueta, too? Or was their place here, at the other end of the table?

Raquel shrugged. She didn't know, either.

Fortunately, Sylvia answered their silent questions. "Kel, Lu, get in here," she said. Together, they slid out of their chairs and made their way toward Sylvia's open arms.

"I want you to meet Lucinda and Raquel," Sylvia said, standing between them and placing a hand first on Lu's shoulder, and then Raquel's. "These are the ones I've told you all about."

Tía Enriqueta squeezed their hands. "It is good to finally meet you," she said. She turned and looked at Dad, her lips pressed together. "It is good to meet *all* of you," she said, and quickly looked away. "Bienvenidos."

Elena began to clap, and the rest of the guests joined. Then Mateo asked, "*Now* can we eat?"

Laughter rose from the table as guests began passing bowls and plates, and the chatter resumed. Even the burbling of the fountain at the center of the patio sounded like it was part of the conversation.

Dad pulled out Tía Enriqueta's chair, but she didn't move to sit down.

"Tía, siéntese," Sylvia said. "Save your strength for the wedding."

Dad tapped the back of the chair. "That's right," he said. "Sylvia has told me what a good dancer you are. I'm hoping you'll save a couple of songs for me."

Raquel was about to go back to her seat, but now she watched as Tía Enriqueta reached for the garnet-studded cross that hung around her neck from a silver chain. She twirled it between her fingers, before clearing her throat.

Once again, the table went quiet. Everyone turned toward Tía Enriqueta.

"Thank you for coming home," she said. "I have felt like a part of my heart was missing this past year."

Someone clinked a spoon against the side of a glass to start a toast. But Tía Enriqueta wasn't finished. Raquel held her breath. Something wasn't right.

"But a marriage?" Tía Enriqueta continued. "It's too soon. This time you have spent together, it hasn't been . . . normal. You are not a family yet. I will not be at the wedding."

11

Lucinda touched the red rose tucked behind her ear. She had taken it from the bud vase on her desk as a last-minute addition to her outfit that afternoon. At the time, it had seemed festive. But now, on this suddenly silent patio, it felt too loud. Like in those panic dreams where she walked in late to a science test inexplicably wearing one of her glittering figure skating dresses. Like everyone was staring at her, even though no one was. The tardeada guests, whose gazes had been fixed on the head of the table only a moment ago, were now looking in every direction *but* theirs.

Some took nervous sips of water while others crumpled their napkins in their laps. Lucinda wished one of them would say something. *Anything.* That way, she could melt back into the noise the way she usually did at big family parties when she wanted to dodge attention.

Even Dad had taken a step backward and seemed to be studying his shoes. But there was nowhere for him to hide, either.

Sylvia cracked a small, brittle smile. "Tía?" she asked. "What do you mean? Don't joke around like that. You're making me nervous."

Her eyes flitted from face to face, as if she was waiting for someone to finally shout "Surprise!" or "Got you!" and reveal the prank. But no one did. One of her uncles coughed into his napkin.

Lucinda slid her foot toward Dad, hoping to slip behind him. But Jules touched her elbow, stopping her. "Don't worry," she said, forcing a laugh. "She's always teasing us. Right, Tía?"

Lucinda wanted to laugh with Jules, but this didn't

feel like a joke. And if it *was* teasing, it was the absolute worst kind.

Tía Enriqueta smoothed the front of her emerald-green blouse.

"I hoped to have a moment to talk with you alone, but there hasn't been time. Everything is moving so fast," she said, as if she were talking only to the two of them. Lucinda's heart sped, each thump urging her to leave, insisting that she didn't belong there. "Too fast."

Sylvia's smile flattened. Jules shook her head. "No," she said, as if she could stop her great-aunt from going any further, as if she could make her take it all back.

But Tía Enriqueta went on. "I told Elena I would keep it to myself, but how can I?"

She turned to Dad. "Please understand," she said to him. "My nieces have been through so much. I only want what's best for them. Sylvia doesn't truly know you yet. The *family* doesn't know—"

Sylvia had been shielding her eyes behind clenched fists, but now she dropped her hands. "If you wanted what was best for us, you would support my choices and my happiness!" she interrupted. "I *don't* understand."

She turned and strode across the patio garden and out toward the grassy ranchland.

"Sylvia!" Dad called after her. Sensing he was about to follow, Lucinda grabbed his arm. But she couldn't stop him. "I'll be right back, mija," he said, then jogged to catch up.

Tía Enriqueta watched them leave, her jaw tight—then she, too, turned and left the patio.

All of a sudden, the burbling fountain seemed too noisy. The clouds on the horizon that had just begun to turn pinkish-orange were too vibrant. The scent of the night-blooming jasmine that grew in clay pots at the edges of the patio was giving Lucinda a headache.

After what felt like hours, Elena pierced the stunned and awkward silence. "I . . . I . . ." she began shakily. "I am sure everything will be all right. My mother . . . she just needs some . . . time. I'll go check on her, but the rest of you, please eat. Provecho."

One by one, the guests obeyed. Forks scraped plates, and ice cubes cracked as water and aguas frescas poured into glasses again. Quiet chatter began to fill the space, though the table was still hushed and uneasy. Carrying on with dinner as if the past few minutes hadn't happened was at least one way to avoid the awful moment they had all shared.

But there was no way Lucinda could go back to her seat at the table now. Her shoulders tensed. Her knees locked.

"Kel, what do we do?" she asked through clenched teeth.

Raquel didn't hesitate. "My room." She took Lucinda's wrist and started back toward the house. Lucinda followed, relieved to have somewhere else to be.

But then she felt Jules's hand at her elbow again.

"Hold on," Jules said.

Lucinda stopped. Raquel turned around sharply. "We're *going*," she said, eyes flashing.

"I'm calling a family meeting," Jules said. "We need to talk. *All* of us. I know where we can go."

Raquel's feet remained firmly planted on the patio's red-orange tiles. "Lu, come on."

"Please?" Jules argued. "Trust me."

Lucinda stood between them, dreading the choice they were forcing her into. She turned to Raquel. She could sense her sister's frustration like the heat from a campfire when you stood too close. Raquel wanted her to follow—*expected* her to follow—but they couldn't just abandon Juliette here on the patio.

"Listen, Kel," she said, barely able to get the words out. "Whatever just happened, it happened to Jules, too." Jules was as much a part of this mess as they were, wasn't she?

"Fine," Raquel said. "Maybe *she* can explain what's going on. But can we please get out of here? *Now?*"

"It's not far," Jules said. She looked down at their feet. "Your shoes might get a little dirty, though. Follow me."

12

The sun was beginning to sink, and Raquel made mental notes of the shrubs and manzanita trees they passed in case she needed to find her way to the house again. She glanced back toward the patio, where golden light glinted off the olive leaves, to gauge how far they'd already walked.

"Are you *sure* you know where you're going?" she asked Jules.

Jules *seemed* sure, marching ahead of them with the same easy confidence that Raquel and Lu had back in

Lockeford. For a moment, Raquel wondered if this was what it had felt like for Jules, following the twins through unfamiliar territory and—as much as she trusted them—having to ignore the nagging worry that she'd be lost and left behind.

"Of course I'm sure," Jules answered. "I could find my way around this ranch in the dark."

That's exactly what they'd have to do if she didn't stop soon.

Raquel reached for her notebook. But then she remembered that the dress she was wearing didn't have pockets, and she'd left the notebook back on the desk in the study. She wanted to write down Tía Enriqueta's exact words so that she'd remember them when she could finally sit and think through what had happened.

Not that she could forget them if she tried.

Not a family yet.

The whole trip suddenly felt like a trap. Sylvia and Jules had led them here, promising a magical time on the family ranch. And Elena and the rest of the relatives had thrown open the doors with so much openhearted kindness that Raquel had almost begun to feel like she was actually a part of this family.

Until Tía Enriqueta slammed those doors shut again.

Just as Raquel was ready to turn around and go back to the house on her own, Jules stopped at the edge of an apple orchard. "Right through here," she said. Then she frowned at the tangle of dry and overgrown branches in front of them, only a few with any fruit. "It's not usually so . . . overgrown."

Raquel snapped off a twig that poked her shoulder. "How long has it been since your family pruned these?" she couldn't help asking.

"They're doing the best they can," Jules said. "These past few months haven't been easy. Things will go back to the way they used to be soon. You've never been here when business is good. You've never been here at all."

Lu tensed. "Jules," she said softly. "She didn't mean anything by it."

"Fine. Sorry," Jules mumbled.

Raquel didn't know as much about trees as Dad did, but she was sure this mess of snarled leaves and branches had taken more than a few months to grow. "Dad would have—"

Lu let out a quiet whine of complaint—a sound a lot like Crybaby made.

"Kel, *please*, is pruning really what you want to talk about right now?" she asked, hugging herself tightly even though the air was dry and warm.

"Sorry," Raquel said reluctantly. "So, now what?"

Jules began carefully pushing aside branches and kicking leaves to make her way through to the center of the orchard. "Over here," she said.

Lu paused and looked to Raquel. *What do you think?* she seemed to ask.

"Vamos," Raquel said. They had already come this far, and now she was beginning to wonder what was behind those trees.

They followed Jules, shoes sinking into a blanket of leaves, until they reached a tree that was taller than the others and had a wooden tree house built into its branches. The pink walls—the same color as the ranch house—were faded and chipped. Long, curling morning glory vines, their blooms already closed for the night, crawled up the sides and into the windows.

Lu stood at the bottom of a frayed rope ladder that led up to the platform on which the house was built. "Are you sure it's safe?" she asked. "It looks a little old."

"Of course it's safe," Jules replied, an impatient edge in her voice. She was already climbing. "Would I bring you here if it wasn't?"

"No," Lu admitted. She waited until Jules had reached the top, then grabbed either side of the ladder and pulled herself up. Raquel took one more look around the orchard, cracked her knuckles, and started climbing, too.

Inside the tree house, Jules opened a chest and pulled out a thick wool blanket with red, purple, and white stripes. She spread it out over the rough floorboards for them to sit on. The planks creaked as she stood again and reached for something on a shelf, just above eye level—a candle and a box of matches. She lit the candle, then placed it on an overturned fruit crate at the center of the room. It filled the space with a soft yellow glow.

"This is nice," Lu said, settling back against one of the walls.

"It is, isn't it?" Jules agreed, looking around the room. "Tía Enriqueta had it built for Mom and Elena when they were little. She kept it up for me and my cousins. We used to spend all day out here. Sometimes all night, too."

Leaves rustled outside the window, and Raquel could imagine that when the orchard was cleaned up—when the smell of apples blew through on the breeze—this would be the perfect place to sit and work on her newspaper stories.

As long as a massive family disaster wasn't waiting for her right outside, of course.

"So," Jules said, focusing their attention again. "How are we going to get Marcos on Tía Enriqueta's good side?"

Raquel's head snapped toward Jules, apple-scented daydreams evaporating. "On *her* good side?" she asked. "*She's* the one who owes Dad an apology. She hasn't even given him a chance."

Jules stood again. She paced to the other side of the tree

house, careful to step around the candle. "It's not that," she said. "Tía Enriqueta, she's just . . . overprotective. We should have known it was going to take time for her to trust you and Marcos, to see you as part of the family."

Raquel could no longer ignore the prickly thought that had been pestering her for most of the afternoon. "Well, it's not like you're helping."

Jules froze in the middle of her pacing. "What are you talking about?"

Lu bit her thumbnail and looked away, out the little tree house window.

"I'm talking about what you said earlier, in the kitchen," Raquel said. "Why did you tell everyone what happened with your mom's cake and the garlic powder? That was ages ago."

"Exactly," Jules replied, pulling off her braided-leather headband and shaking out her hair. "It was a long time ago, and it's *funny*. I thought we could laugh about it now. It doesn't *mean* anything."

Raquel was not convinced that Jules really thought it was funny. She stood, too. "But what if they told Tía

Enriqueta about it? It wouldn't give her a very good impression of us."

Jules took a step forward. "You think she didn't know already? Mom and Cousin Elena talk *all* the time. It's not my fault that you didn't exactly welcome Mom and me when we first met. You can't blame Tía Enriqueta for worrying."

"So it's true," Raquel said, putting a hand on her hip. "You still hold it against me." Usually she loved this moment in an interview, when someone revealed the innermost thoughts they had been trying to keep secret. But this time, it just felt dull and heavy. Like seeing the F on a test you knew you hadn't studied for. It wasn't a surprise, but that didn't stop the ache of it.

"Stop! *Please!*" Lu jumped and stood between them. "Please," she repeated. "Don't fight." She twisted one of her curls.

Raquel swallowed. She forced her breath to slow and wished she hadn't mentioned the kitchen incident after all.

"We're a team. We can fix this?" It wasn't a question,

but the soft and uncertain way Lu spoke made it sound like one.

"I thought that's why we were here," Jules said. "It's why *I'm* here anyway."

They both looked at Raquel.

"Me too." She dropped back down to the wool blanket. "So. We have less than a week to change Tía Enriqueta's mind and get her to come to the wedding. Do either of you have any great ideas?"

They didn't answer. As usual, it would be up to Raquel to figure out a plan. Only, she wasn't having any more luck finding great ideas here than she had back in Lockeford.

But then Lu reached out the window and twisted off a small apple, still pale green and unripe. She brought it to her nose and sniffed. "I might have one."

13

She had to set an alarm to be sure she got to Dad and Sylvia early, before anyone else was awake to overhear, especially Tía Enriqueta. After silencing her cell phone's insistent chirp, Lucinda yawned and opened a text message she had missed the day before. It was from the animal shelter volunteer who was taking care of Crybaby. She sent a picture of him, sprawled in a patch of sunlight, batting lazily at a tangle of yarn. Lucinda smiled. This was a sign, she decided. Everything was going to work out all right in the end. They would be able to unsnarl this mess that they hadn't realized they were tangled up in to begin with.

She got dressed, then tapped on Jules's door.

"Why didn't you use the tunnel?" Jules whispered. "It would have been quieter."

The truth was, she'd thought about it, but the idea made her feel slightly guilty. Like the tunnel was something they were keeping from Raquel. She couldn't tell Jules that, though. She shrugged. "Guess I forgot."

Together, the two of them tiptoed out to the patio, where Jules said Sylvia always spent her mornings when they visited Flor de Manzana.

The banquet table from the night before had been cleared away. Dad sat drinking his coffee on the bricks that surrounded the fountain. Sylvia was near, clipping roses and dropping them into a woven straw basket. A silky blue scarf held her hair off her face.

"Morning," Lucinda said softly, hesitant to disturb the quiet. Sylvia smiled, but not quite as brightly as usual.

"You're up early," Dad said. "Where's your sister? She's the one who usually can't stay in bed past sunrise."

Jules dug her hands into the pockets of her cutoff jean shorts. "We tried to get her to come out," she said. "But she's . . . working on something."

"A story," Lucinda added. That's what Raquel had told her anyway, and she hoped it was true. Still, she couldn't help worrying that Tía Enriqueta wasn't the only one who needed to be convinced they were really a family.

"That's so good to hear," Sylvia said, smiling again, this time with her usual dazzle. But it faded quickly. "I'll take any good news at the moment."

"Does that mean you haven't talked to Tía Enriqueta yet?" Jules asked.

Sylvia walked over to the fountain and balanced the basket of roses on the bricks. She rested her hand on Dad's shoulder, and he put his on top of it. Obviously, they had been waiting for this conversation.

"Not since last night," Sylvia said. "I think maybe she needs some time. I've given it a lot of thought, and I can understand how this might have seemed very sudden to her. But I know she'll come around once she sees . . ."

The sentence hung in the air unfinished. As if not

even Sylvia had figured out what might convince Tía Enriqueta to change her mind. A new wave of worry washed over Lucinda. If Sylvia wasn't sure, how could the rest of them be?

Still, Lucinda forced herself to swim against her doubts. "We have a plan!" she announced.

Dad shook his head slowly. "Mija, I know you want to help, but—"

"Just *listen*," Jules interrupted. "It's a good plan. Lucinda came up with it."

Dad set his coffee mug beside him on the bricks. *"Lucinda?"* he asked, not even trying to hide his surprise. Usually it was Raquel who came up with all their schemes. But why shouldn't Lucinda have a plan? Why shouldn't she be the one to keep the family moving in the right direction? She met Dad's eyes and nodded.

"We were in the apple orchard yesterday, and it's really overgrown, like they haven't been able to prune in a while," Lucinda began.

Jules chimed in. "Alejandra told us business has been slow. They can't hire as many workers."

Sylvia's forehead wrinkled. "Elena did mention—"

Lucinda took a breath. "Well, I . . . *we* . . . thought maybe you could prune them, Dad. It would help the family *and* show Tía Enriqueta that you care about the ranch, too."

Dad and Sylvia leaned forward, waiting for Lucinda to say more, but there wasn't any more to say.

"Well, um, that's pretty much it," she finished. "That's my plan." It seemed much smaller than it had in the tree house. Almost silly. Lucinda turned her head down and jostled a broken piece of tile with the toe of her sandal.

"I bet Elena would appreciate the help," Sylvia said finally.

Lucinda lifted her eyes. "Really?"

Jules squealed. She took Lucinda's hand and squeezed.

Lucinda wasn't going to celebrate until Dad said yes. He smiled up at Sylvia, then ran a hand through his hair. "I would be happy to help, but we've never grown apples at Los Robles."

"But you know how to take care of all kinds of trees," Lucinda pleaded. "You must have learned *something* about apples."

Maybe it was because he was as desperate to solve this problem as the rest of them were. Or maybe it was just that he still wasn't used to taking time off and liked the idea of a project. But when Dad looked around at the three of them, Lucinda noticed a glimmer of adventure—like the one that had brought them to Mexico—in his eyes.

"It can't hurt to take a look."

Lucinda checked her phone one last time to see if Raquel had replied to the fourth text she'd sent, begging her to join them.

She hadn't. So while Dad called one of his friends back in Lockeford for advice on pruning apple trees, Lucinda went with Jules and Sylvia to a storage shed where they found gloves and tools tidily organized on hooks and pegs.

When they met back up in the golden morning sunlight, the orchard looked even more neglected than it had the evening before.

Dad shielded his eyes with his hand while he studied the trees.

Sylvia stood beside him. "I've been picking apples here

since I was a little girl," she said. "I hate to see it like this when I know how beautiful it could be."

Dad picked up a saw. "We'll fix this," he said. Lucinda wasn't sure whether he was still talking about the apple trees or something bigger. But if he believed they could do it, then she did, too. She followed him into the trees with a set of clippers and watched him work.

"We don't want to cut too much," he explained. "It's not the right time of year. But we can start by clearing out any dead or broken branches. That will help."

They didn't stop until hours later when their stomachs began growling. Lucinda's shoulders ached. She had leaves in her hair and mud on her shoes. Still, she felt better walking back to the house than she had leaving it that morning.

Elena was laying out lunch when they got to the kitchen.

"Food!" Jules exclaimed, eyes wide. She dove for one of the bolillos left over from the day before.

Tía Enriqueta, who had been arranging the roses Sylvia gathered, chuckled to herself.

But when she saw them, all sweaty and full of dust, she wrinkled her nose.

"¿Qué han estado haciendo?" she asked.

Sylvia grinned. "We've been pruning your apple trees," she said. "It looked like you needed some help, and Marcos here is an expert." She patted his shoulder while he bent to take off his shoes before stepping inside.

"This is beautiful land," Dad said to Tía Enriqueta as he straightened.

She tucked another rose into the vase, then added a sprig of lavender. "I don't remember Sylvia telling me that you grow apples in California."

Jules stopped chewing. Lucinda sucked in a breath.

"Pues," Dad began, "we don't—"

Tía Enriqueta didn't let him finish. "You don't grow apples?" she asked, turning to him. "And yet you come here and think you can cut mine?" She set down the flowers and narrowed her eyes. "You think you can take over? My grandfather planted those trees. You might have damaged them."

For a second, Lucinda thought she felt the floor shake,

but it was only her knees wobbling. She wanted to escape back into the orchard, but she couldn't let Tía Enriqueta blame Dad for this. It had been *her* idea.

"It . . . it . . . wasn't my dad's fault," she started. "I was the one who—"

Sylvia stepped forward before she could continue. "Tía, you are being very unfair. Marcos was only trying—"

"And you are rushing into things as usual," Tía Enriqueta interrupted again. "Without thinking about the consequences. We can't afford to have anything else go wrong at this ranch. We'll lose everything. I don't expect *him* to understand." She nodded toward Dad. "But I thought you would be more careful. I thought you would protect your family."

Sylvia took another step forward. "Marcos is my family," she said.

Tía Enriqueta shook her head. She picked up another rose stem and stripped away its thorns with the swipe of a dish towel.

14

Raquel could tell that Jules and Lucinda didn't completely believe her when she explained why she wasn't going to help them prune the trees. They suspected Raquel was up to something. They weren't wrong. But they didn't know *what* she was up to.

The truth was, neither did Raquel exactly. Not yet.

She went over Tía Enriqueta's words from the tardeada for what might have been the thousandth time. As predicted, she remembered the speech with perfect clarity even though she hadn't been able to jot it down in her notebook. Now that she wasn't on the patio, with dozens of eyes on her, it was easier to take the words apart.

You're not a family yet.

Raquel doubted Tía Enriqueta would have said that if she had been with them in Lockeford these past months. If she had seen for herself the way Mom and Dad and Sylvia had set aside their feelings so they could all be near one another during the most difficult days of the pandemic. The way they had pulled together through worries and frustrations and disappointments—as well as unexpected moments of celebration.

It wasn't only Tía Enriqueta's words that Raquel remembered clearly. She could also close her eyes and picture the way Tía Enriqueta had clenched her jaw, how her voice had wavered when she said she wouldn't attend the wedding. Perhaps she hated letting Sylvia down the way Raquel hated to disappoint Lucinda that morning.

Yet she had done it anyway. She must have believed it was for the best.

Helping out with chores on the ranch might not hurt,

Raquel thought after Lu explained her plan. But it wouldn't change Tía Enriqueta's mind.

"She doesn't know us," Raquel whispered to herself. That was the real problem.

And despite what she'd thought earlier, Raquel realized they didn't know Tía Enriqueta, either. But if she could understand Tía Enriqueta and how her mind worked, she might be able to figure out what it would take to show her they belonged in this family. It was a job for an investigative journalist, she decided, fingers twitching with eagerness to begin. The only question was *where*.

Raquel stood, pen tucked behind her ear, in front of the bookcases. She was tempted to reach for another volume in the mystery series, or one of the fairy-tale collections from the row above. Perhaps Tía Enriqueta had underlined passages or left notes in the margins. Clues about her likes and dislikes and the kinds of characters she admired.

But then Raquel's glance drifted to that odd mirror near the window. Reflected in it was what looked like an even older book with a brown leather cover and bits of paper poking out from between the pages. "A scrapbook?"

She found it in the bookcase on the opposite side of the room and carried it to the bed, cradled in both arms. The cover left a dusty film on her palms, as if it hadn't been disturbed in many years. Raquel clapped the dust off, sneezed, and opened the book in her lap, notepad beside her.

Black-and-white photos, like the ones she had seen in the hallway, were pasted into the first few pages. One showed a family picnicking on top of a car, laughing as they popped grapes into their mouths. Written neatly in the thin white border was the name of a lake, Laguna de Encinillas, that Raquel remembered driving past a few days before.

On the next page was a photo of the apple orchard when it was newly planted, the same family posing proudly in front of the saplings. Raquel recognized Tía Enriqueta near the edge of the frame, with her serious and watchful eyes, a little like Jules's. She was there again in the next picture, this one taken outside a church. Tía Enriqueta and another girl, both wearing light-colored dresses with puffed sleeves and short, full skirts, stood behind a cart. According to a hand-painted sign that leaned against it, they were selling obleas.

As Raquel turned the page, something fell onto the quilt beside her. It was a newspaper clipping, the ink beginning to fade. Carefully, she smoothed it and read, pausing only a few times to type words into the Spanish–English dictionary on her phone.

It was a story about a rancher—Tía Enriqueta's grandfather, Raquel guessed, judging by the date—who had just sold his family's recipe for obleas, passed down through generations, to a candy company.

Now people all over Mexico, and maybe even the world, will get to enjoy the delectable flavors that we in Municipio Casas Grandes know so well, the article proclaimed.

So it was true. The Viramontes family *was* famous for its obleas. Raquel was finally onto something. She grabbed the pen from behind her ear and flipped to a blank page in her notepad. She started to write down the date of the article, but her pen only dug scratches into the paper. Out of ink.

Raquel let out an impatient growl. She set the scrapbook down, hopped off the bed, and scrambled to the desk for a fresh pen.

She yanked open the center drawer, but it was empty

except for a worn guest book, some paper clips, and a few loose ten-centavo coins. She reached farther. There *had* to be a pen in there.

Then her knuckles grazed the edge of something solid. Something she didn't expect.

"Hmm . . ." Raquel knelt to peer inside. Near the back was another drawer with a tiny brass keyhole. Raquel tugged, but the drawer didn't budge. Pen forgotten, she snapped up one of the paper clips and unbent it. She obviously couldn't *ignore* a secret compartment. She stuck the paper clip into the keyhole and wiggled it until the lock finally gave with a soft *click*. The drawer slid open.

Raquel held her breath. Inside was a book. Its cloth cover, a little worn, was pale green with tiny white blossoms. She lifted it from the drawer and opened it. At the top of the first page, just like in the mystery novel, Tía Enriqueta had written her name: *Keta*.

And underneath that, printed in gold script, was one word: *Diario*.

Her diary. Raquel looked over her shoulder as if someone might be watching.

She knew she should put the diary back.

She knew she should not turn another page.

She knew she *definitely* shouldn't read any of it.

And yet, the diary had just been sitting there, for who knew how long, for any stranger to find. More importantly, it was the best chance she had of getting inside Tía Enriqueta's head. Almost as if she was meant to find it.

She did not put the diary back. She turned another page, and her eyes raced over the sharply slanted cursive.

As she read, her shoulders—tense with anticipation at first—dropped.

This was not a treasure chest of Tía Enriqueta's innermost thoughts. It was mostly a record of where she had gone and the friends she had seen. Three whole pages were dedicated to the baptism of her baby brother—that must have been Sylvia's dad—and all the guests who had come and the gifts the baby had received and the dishes her mother had served on the patio.

It was . . . boring. Raquel was about to return the diary to the drawer when one last hunch wriggled into her mind.

She flipped ahead, to dates near the one from the newspaper clipping.

That's when she found it. Something worth locking up in a secret drawer.

Today, Abuelo gave an interview about the obleas. They made me stay in my room the whole time. I think they were worried I'd tell the reporter the truth. That the recipe, the one everyone says will make us famous, was <u>stolen</u>!

Raquel gasped. This was better than just a secret. This was a *story*. She bent closer to the page, hungry to read more.

But then she heard a knock.

She slammed the diary shut and slid it across the floor and under the bed.

"Kel?"

Raquel exhaled. It was only Lu.

"Yeah?" she answered, trying to make her voice sound casual. Normal. Not the voice of someone who had uncovered a major family mystery.

"Lunch is ready," Lu replied. It was the voice of someone whose plan had definitely *not* worked.

15

"Horseback riding? *Seriously?*" When she and Raquel were younger, Abuelo would sometimes take them to neighboring farms to ride when they visited Lockeford for the summer. Under normal circumstances, Lucinda would have loved to be on a horse again. But nothing was normal now. They had a wedding to save. And it was only going to be harder after her idea had turned into such a spectacular failure yesterday.

"Shouldn't we be getting ready for the wedding?" Lucinda asked. "There's so much to do. Cooking?

Cleaning? Decorating?" Behind those questions was another that she was too afraid to ask: *There's still going to be a wedding, right?*

But Dad and Sylvia were already walking toward the stable, boots crunching in the red dirt. "Vamos," Dad said without looking back. "We could all use some fresh air."

What they could *use* was a new plan, and there would be no time to come up with one if they were out riding all day.

"Raquel, didn't you say you had a schedule to keep?" Raquel always had a schedule. For once, Lucinda could use it to her advantage.

Only Raquel, who usually never hesitated to tell them what they should be doing and when, didn't even look up from her phone screen. "Huh?"

Perfect. She wasn't paying attention. Just like the previous afternoon when she only half listened to Lucinda's retelling of the disastrous pruning incident before shutting herself up in the study for more "research." Raquel was definitely up to something. But Lucinda didn't have time to pry it out of her. She jogged ahead to where Jules was walking.

"We need to call another sisters meeting," she said, keeping her voice low. "We need Kel to help us figure out what to do next."

Jules shrugged. "She didn't help us yesterday," she said. "What makes you think she even *wants* to?"

Before Lucinda could recover from the sting of those words, Jules sped up and ran the rest of the way. "I want to ride Damita!" she yelled.

The horses were in the pasture, grazing in the warm morning sunlight. Luis was there, leaning against the fence while Oso galloped back and forth along its perimeter. "They're all ready for you," he said.

Sylvia kissed his cheek. "Gracias." Oso nuzzled his nose against her knee, and she patted him. "Good morning, Osito, are you ready for a ride?"

Jules scrambled up and over the fence's wooden planks and walked straight to a horse with a cream-colored coat and silvery mane. She pulled an apple from her pocket, and Damita eagerly ate it from her hand. "So you *do* remember me," Jules said, smiling as she patted the horse's shoulder.

Sylvia unlatched the gate.

"Armonia and Octava are over there," she said, pointing at two horses nibbling grass under the feathery green leaves of a mesquite tree. "They're very sweet, and I thought they'd be perfect for you girls. And, Marcos, we saved Cascabel for you."

Dad and Lucinda started to follow Sylvia through the gate and into the pasture, but Raquel didn't move. She had lowered her phone and was staring at Armonia and Octava. Lucinda squinted, trying to see what Raquel saw. The horses were smaller than the ones they had ridden before in Lockeford. But they were still horses, and Raquel was suspicious of things she couldn't control.

"They're so big," Raquel said, her attention finally pulled away from her phone. "I'll stay behind. You guys can go."

"I'll stay with her!" Lucinda volunteered. Jules's head snapped toward them. She scowled and led Damita away. Lucinda's heart sank, but she needed to talk, *really* talk, to Raquel. Jules would understand. Wouldn't she?

But then Dad clapped his arm around Raquel's

shoulder. "Órale, we're in this together now," he said softly. "You've done this before. It'll all come back to you. Just like riding a bike. Vamos, I'll help you up."

The ride started well. Armonia, a pale gray mare, was as gentle as Sylvia promised. Even Raquel settled quickly into the ride, pulling her phone from her pocket to take a picture. "Smile, Octava," she said.

Jules trotted out in front with Sylvia not far behind. Small brown birds twittered in the shrubs on either side of the desert trail, and flew away shrieking when Oso bounded up to them. Sylvia said there was a stream ahead where they could stop for a picnic before riding on to a pottery village nearby. She had packed fresh bolillos and homemade goat cheese sprinkled with herbs.

They didn't get a chance to taste any of it.

Out of nowhere, Dad's horse, Cascabel, stopped in the middle of the trail and refused to take another step forward. Lucinda and Raquel snorted, looking behind them as he desperately tried to convince the horse—first in Spanish, then in English—to move. *Anywhere.*

Then, when Cascabel finally started walking again, it was only to veer off the trail. "¡Para! Stop!" Dad yelled, pulling hopelessly on the reins. Cascabel flicked his ears but otherwise paid no attention.

Sylvia circled back, smiling patiently, and helped Dad steer Cascabel back onto the trail.

But soon, the whole cycle started again.

"You have to be firm and clear, Marcos!" Sylvia said. "Or else he won't listen to you."

"I don't know how to be any clearer!" Dad replied, taking off his baseball hat and running his hand through his hair in frustration.

"Well, maybe we should just turn back."

Dad didn't argue.

The girls let the two of them ride ahead.

"It's hot. Everyone's tired," Raquel said as she watched Sylvia guide Dad and Cascabel home. Even Oso slowed down to a lazy slog, tail drooping. "They'll feel better after we've had a rest."

"And some lunch," Jules added.

Lucinda wasn't sure whether they were trying to

convince her—or *themselves*—that everything was going to be okay. She wouldn't call it a fight. But with a pang, she thought it was the kind of bickering that could turn into one. Worse, Dad and Sylvia were still at it, even after returning the horses to the pasture and making their way to the house.

"I thought you said you could ride," Sylvia said. "If I had known you couldn't, I never would have suggested this."

"I *can* ride," Dad answered. "I'm just used to better-behaved animals."

Sylvia wheeled around. "So now you're saying we don't know how to train our horses?"

Someone coughed, loud enough to distract Dad and Sylvia, and Lucinda was grateful for the interruption.

Until she saw who it was.

Tía Enriqueta stood farther ahead on the path that led to the patio. She was refilling one of the blown-glass hummingbird feeders that hung here and there in the garden.

"Perfect," Lucinda said, aloud this time. Why even

bother trying to keep it to herself? It's not like it could make matters worse now that Dad and Sylvia were basically proving to Tía Enriqueta that she was right about them all along.

Sylvia took off the straw hat she wore and fanned herself with it. "Tía," she said. "You startled me. Shouldn't you be inside the house? It's getting warm out here."

Tía Enriqueta tightened the top of the jewel-toned feeder. "Making sure my birds have food," she said. She hung the feeder from a hook on the wall, and then turned on the hose to fill a bowl of water for Oso. "You've been out riding?"

"Trying to," Jules said.

Tía Enriqueta smirked. "Cascabel?"

"So, the horse has a reputation?" Dad glowered at Sylvia. "You failed to mention that."

Sylvia sniffed. "*I've* never had any trouble with him."

"Pues, I only hope he doesn't give Señor Gutierrez any trouble when he comes to take a look at him next week," Tía Enriqueta said, shaking her head.

"Gutierrez?" Sylvia asked. "The trainer? He's so

expensive. If it helps you save some money, I could spend some time working with Cascabel while we're here—"

"Not to work with him," Tía Enriqueta said, cutting Sylvia off. "To buy him. If we're lucky." She bent to pick up her watering can, then straightened again. "We can't afford the horses. Without any guests, we can barely afford to keep up the house. Señor Gutierrez has known the family a long time. He'll make us a fair offer."

She turned to water a fuchsia that grew in a hanging basket, but Sylvia reached forward and took the can away.

"You can't sell the horses," Sylvia said. "I know it's been difficult, but things are looking better now. And I can help you with marketing. I've told you before, I have so many ideas—"

Tía Enriqueta put up a hand to stop her. "You *don't* know," she said. "You haven't been here." She looked at Dad. "Better we sell the horses than the whole ranch, ¿verdad?"

Jules pushed past Lucinda. "You'd never do that!" A strand of her hair stuck to her tear-streaked cheek.

Tía Enriqueta brushed it away. "Not if I can help it, corazón."

Dad took off his hat. He draped his arm around Sylvia's shoulders. All the annoyance that had sharpened his features only minutes ago softened.

Just as Lucinda's eyes began to prickle, too, she felt Raquel's hand around her elbow, and then a sharp tug toward the house.

16

"My room," Raquel whispered as she and Lu slipped their dusty shoes off at the door. She strode down the hall.

Lu hesitated, socks sliding to a stop on the tile floor. *"Wait!"*

Raquel spun around. "We don't have time. They'll all come inside soon."

Lu glanced behind her, toward the patio and the garden. "What about Jules? Whatever this is, she should hear it, too."

As far as Raquel was concerned, there was only one subject to discuss: the diary and the secret it revealed.

But Lu didn't know about either, and Raquel needed to talk to her before they broke the news to Jules.

"She'll find us," Raquel replied. Then, before Lu could worry them into another moment of delay, Raquel took her elbow again and practically dragged her the rest of the way to the old study. *"Hurry."*

She pulled open the door and, once Lu was inside, slammed it shut behind them.

"So," Lu breathed out in a puff. "You have a plan? I knew you'd think of something. I *told* Jules you would. What is it? What are we going to do?" She was bouncing on her toes. Her eyes were wide and hopeful.

Raquel scrunched her nose. "A plan?"

Lu stopped bouncing. She threw up her arms in frustration. Frazzled curls had escaped her bun. "A plan to convince Tía Enriqueta to come to the wedding, obviously. *Nothing* is working. Things are even worse than they were before, and we're running out of time."

Ignoring Lu's panic, Raquel sat at the writing desk and opened the middle drawer, where she'd returned the diary after reading it cover to cover. Slowly, she pulled it out.

"This is even better than a plan," she said, gazing down at it. "It's a *story*, and it might be exactly what we need."

Lu stepped closer to the desk. "Wh-what do you mean? What is it?"

Raquel could hear the shake in her voice. Lu was nervous. But then she was always nervous at the beginnings of things. Carefully, as if it might burn her, Lucinda reached out a finger to touch the cover.

Raquel pushed the diary toward her. "Open it."

Lucinda turned to a page near the beginning. She read, her lips moving as she worked to translate the loopy Spanish cursive. "This morning was the birthday of my friend..." She stopped and frowned. "Kel, this seems like..." She dropped her voice to a frantic hiss. "Raquel, is this someone's *diary*?"

Raquel took the diary back from her, smiling. Lu had missed the most important part. As usual. "Not just *any* someone," she said, opening the front cover. She pointed to the name written in the top corner, the swooping *K*, the towering *t*.

"It's Tía Enriqueta's."

Lu clapped her hand over her mouth. She glanced toward the door. It was still shut.

"Put that away!" she said through her fingers. "Where did you take it from?"

Raquel should have known Lu would react this way. She tried to keep her voice steady and even. "I didn't *take* it," she explained. "It was just . . . here. I found it last night when I was looking for a pen."

Lu blew out a breath in relief. "Well, you didn't read it, did you?"

Raquel knew she was being serious—this was Lu, after all—but it was still hard to believe. How could you possibly find something like this and put it back without a closer look? "Of *course* I read it."

"*Kel!*"

"What?"

"You can't go around reading people's diaries," Lu said. She bit the edge of her thumbnail. "Everyone knows that. It's, like, a basic rule or something."

She had a point. But Raquel had convinced herself

that there were exceptions to that rule, and one was that a diary older than she was didn't count. The person who wrote it was someone completely different now.

"Don't you want to hear what I found out?"

Lu folded her arms across her chest. "No," she said.

Raquel raised an eyebrow. *"Really?"*

"Fine," Lu said. "Not like I could stop you from telling me anyway."

Raquel carried the diary over to the bed and flopped onto the quilt. Lu sat beside her. She took one of the patchwork throw pillows and hugged it against her chest. Raquel was certain that if Crybaby had been there, Lu would have wrestled him onto her lap for support.

Raquel knew her sister wouldn't sit still very long, not when she was so anxious. She flipped straight to the page she had discovered yesterday and had reread dozens of times since. She pointed to the words that now stood out to her like they were flashing in neon.

...the recipe, the one everyone says will make us famous, was stolen!

Lu took the diary from her hands and pulled it close. Raquel watched her eyebrows crinkle as she tried to make sense of it.

"Recipe," Lu said. "Stolen."

Raquel had to bite her lip to keep from bursting. When she couldn't stand it anymore, she blurted, "Don't you get it? That recipe—for the obleas—that Sylvia and Jules are always talking about, the one their family sold to the candy company? It wasn't theirs. It was stolen!"

Lu shook her head. "No. That can't be true. They're famous for it."

Raquel took the diary back and tapped on the page. "But there it is. And Tía Enriqueta would know, wouldn't she? I've cross-referenced the dates with some family pictures, and I'm pretty sure they used the money from the recipe sale to plant the apple orchard. It must have been worth a lot." She paused. What she hadn't figured out yet was why Tía Enriqueta's diary entry had seemed so angry. And why would her grandfather worry that she would reveal the truth?

Still, she said, more to herself than to Lu, "We can use

this." She didn't know where the thought would lead, but she was willing to follow. "Maybe Tía Enriqueta would back off if she knew that *we* knew the ranch was built on a lie."

Lu jumped off the bed. "No," she said, more firmly than Raquel had ever heard her speak before. "We can't. Think of how Jules would feel if she found out. *Please.* Promise me you won't say anything. We can't tell her."

The door creaked. Raquel shoved the diary under a pillow.

"Can't tell me what?" Jules asked.

17

Lucinda's cheeks went hot as she tried to force words—any words—out of her mouth. None would come. She could only stare, open-mouthed, at Jules. *How much did she hear? How much did she see?*

Jules stared back, her eyes red and puffy from crying. She took another step into the room. "Tell me *what*?" she asked again.

Raquel slid over, putting herself between Jules and what Lucinda knew was the diary. It was hopeless. In Lucinda's imagination the diary might as well have been alive with blinking lights and blaring sirens, refusing to be hidden.

Somehow, Raquel stayed calm. "Lu was making me promise not to tell our *mom* what happened with the apple orchard," she said. "The whole pruning idea. Mom told us no more scheming, so . . ."

Jules looked from Raquel to Lucinda. "Lu?" she asked. But what Lucinda heard was *You don't actually expect me to believe that, do you?*

The lie sat on Lucinda's chest like a boulder. Yet she couldn't tell Jules the truth. The truth was even worse. She turned her eyes down to the quilt and traced her fingers over the stitching. She nodded.

Jules paused before replying, giving Lucinda one last chance to change her mind. But she didn't. She couldn't.

"Anyway, it's time to milk the goats," Jules said finally, disappointment flattening her voice. "I came to see if you wanted to help. But you don't have to if you don't want to. Or if you're busy or whatever."

Anything to get out of this room and away from the diary. "We'll help," Lucinda said.

"So, you want to go for a jog around the ranch later?" Lucinda asked Jules, as if everything was normal between them. Even though nothing was. She knew Jules was angry. She knew she deserved it. Still, she could pretend she didn't notice Jules's icy silence as they followed Sarita and Alejandra to the goat pen. She could *pretend* everything was okay. And maybe, if she pretended hard enough, Jules would believe it, too. "Or we could go looking for some plants to turn into dyes?"

"I don't know," Jules said. "It's pretty hot out here." Then she quickened her pace to catch up with her cousins, leaving Lucinda behind.

"She's worried about losing the ranch, that's all," Raquel said quietly when Jules was far enough away not to hear.

That's all? It was plenty, but it wasn't *all*. Getting Tía Enriqueta to the wedding seemed even more important than ever, knowing it might be their only chance to create a family memory at this place that meant so much to Jules and Sylvia. Yet saving the wedding wasn't any simpler than saving the ranch.

Lucinda swallowed. Neither was saving their sisterhood.

They reached the pen, a rectangular patch of dirt and grass near the apple orchard. Alejandra stood on tiptoe to unlock the gate. Six goats rested inside. They rose and trotted forward, *baa*-ing impatiently when the girls entered.

"Don't worry, we'll get to all of you," Sarita said, sweeping her long black hair into a ponytail.

One of the goats—they stood no taller than the girls' knees—nuzzled Lucinda's palm. "Oh, hello!" She jumped. "¡Mucho gusto!"

Jules latched the gate behind them. "Who's fi-irst?" she warbled.

One of the smaller goats, with black and brown splotches on her white coat, tilted her head up at Jules. *Maaaa.*

Jules laughed and scratched the goat's head. "I don't think I've met you before. What's your name?"

Sarita was already helping her sister fasten a rope halter around the neck of a black goat with white ears.

She glanced back at Jules and grimaced. "That's Canicas," she said. "We call her that because her coloring looks like the inside of a marble. Be careful. She likes to kick."

Raquel took a big step away from Canicas, but Jules dropped to her knees and patted the goat's neck. "You look like a good girl. You won't kick me, right?"

Alejandra ducked into a shed at the far end of the pen and came back with two aluminum pails and two clean towels. She brought them over to Jules. "Suerte," she said. "We're taking Luna. She's calmer." Together, Sarita and Alejandra led Luna onto a raised platform. Then Sarita dragged a three-legged stool up beside it.

"Get me a rope?" Jules said, looking over at Lucinda. "There should be another one in the shed."

"*Yes!*" Lucinda replied, with more enthusiasm than was probably necessary. She was just so relieved Jules had spoken to her—that there was something she could do to help. She raced to the shed.

"Oh, and a scoopful of oats," Jules added. "We'll put some in the feeder on the milking stand. That should keep Canicas occupied for a while. And, Kel, could you soak the towel?" She pointed to the spigot poking out of the dirt next to a fence post.

"Sure," Raquel answered. Lucinda wished she could have at least *tried* to sound more excited about it, but at least they were cooperating again.

Lucinda returned with a rope in one hand and an old soup can filled with oats in the other. After showing Lucinda where to pour the oats into the feeder, Jules looped the rope gently over the goat's head the same way Sarita had. Then, the halter secure, she led Canicas over to an empty milk stand and up its short ramp.

Once she was settled, Canicas bleated happily and dipped her snout in the feeder. Jules took the damp towel from Raquel and used it to wipe the goat's udder.

Finally, she sat on the stool, reached underneath Canicas, and squirted some milk into the dirt.

"Ergh!" Raquel jumped backward—and surprisingly high. She should really give figure skating another chance, Lucinda thought.

It was enough to make Jules laugh. "It's only milk," she said. "It's not going to hurt you." She stood. "You try."

Raquel shook her head. "No, thanks. I should probably watch you some more," she said, wrinkling her nose and waving vaguely at Canicas. "I don't want to break anything."

Sarita and Alejandra watched from the other milking stand.

"It's really not that hard," Jules said.

Lucinda winced. This could turn out badly. Another jamaica incident that started with smiles but ended with a sting. The thing was, she wanted to trust Jules.

She decided she would.

"Go on, Kel," Lucinda urged, betting on the one challenge she knew her sister could not possibly turn down. "I bet *Paul Campos* would do it. I bet he'd write a first-person essay for the homepage of the *Mirror*."

It worked.

"Fine." Raquel glared at her, then took Jules's place on the stool. "So, what now?"

Jules set the pail under Canicas. She stood at Raquel's

side. "You're just going to squeeze here," she said, guiding Raquel's hand. "Go ahead."

Raquel turned her head away from Canicas. She squinched her eyes shut and squeezed. A splash of milk landed in the pail with a soft ping.

"I did it!" Raquel said, opening her eyes and gazing into the pail. "It worked!" She squeezed again.

"Told you it wasn't hard," Jules said.

But then Canicas bleated and raised one of her back legs.

"Watch out!" Jules shouted. She snatched the pail away just as Canicas kicked.

"What happened? What did I do?" Raquel asked, jumping off the stool.

Jules stroked the goat's shoulder and made a shushing noise. "It's not you," she told Raquel. "Some of them are more nervous than others." She scratched Canicas between the ears. "But we still love you, don't we? Are you ready to try again?"

"I think it's Lu's turn," Raquel said, pushing her forward.

Before Lucinda could protest, the gate clanged.

Tía Enriqueta stood inside the pen, squinting in the sun.

"Julieta," she said. "Come inside when you're finished, eh? I have something I want to give you and your mother."

18

Questions

Where did cajeta come from originally?

Where did the family recipe go?

Why is Tía Enriqueta the only one who knows it?

Lu and Raquel lugged the two heavy pails back to the house when the milking was finished.

By then, it was late afternoon. The sunlight, which had been so harsh earlier, had begun to turn a mellow gold. While the others raced ahead, Lu and Raquel walked slowly, careful not to spill any of the milk. The distance gave Raquel time to think about something she first realized back in the goat pen. In all the black-and-white pictures of the ranch, it was only Tía Enriqueta who ever appeared with the goats. Maybe, like Sarita and Alejandra, she was the one who cared for them. Who collected the milk for the cajeta. Maybe she—

"What do you think Tía Enriqueta is going to give Jules and Sylvia?" Lu asked, interrupting Raquel's thoughts. "Do you think it's her *blessing*? Maybe she finally decided to come to the wedding after all!"

Raquel did *not* think it was her blessing. Someone who had stubbornly kept a secret for as long as Tía Enriqueta had would not give in so easily. But Raquel could see how desperate Lu was to believe it was possible. "Maybe?" she answered. "I guess we're about to find out."

They had reached the door that led into the kitchen. They took off their shoes, then went inside, where Cousin Elena had already begun to prepare dinner.

"Ah, gracias," she said. "Leave the milk on the counter. I need to heat it so it's safe to drink." She nodded toward another doorway. "They're waiting for you."

Lu gave Raquel's hand a squeeze. She leaned in and squealed softly in Raquel's ear. "I hope it's good news!"

Now that she had studied so many pictures of the property's earlier days, Raquel knew that the cavernous room they stepped into had once been where the Viramontes family—and all people who worked on the ranch—ate lunches and dinners. And that, at least sometimes, when there was a celebration, someone would play the guitar in front of the big tiled fireplace while the others danced and clapped.

The room wasn't so full this evening, Raquel observed. But it was just as warm as in the photographs. Jules and Sarita sprawled on one of the worn leather sofas, while Alejandra lounged in a matching armchair and Oso snored on a rug. At a small round table, Dad and Mateo, faces tense with concentration, were building a tower out of lotería cards. Sylvia sat next to them with her laptop open. Raquel looked over her shoulder.

"Tourism forecast," she read aloud.

Sylvia startled and clicked the tab closed. "Just trying to get some ideas for marketing the ranch," she said with a sigh. Raquel nodded. It's what she would have done. What she was *always* trying to do: get to the bottom of things, find out as much as she could in order to come up with a plan.

Sylvia rubbed the bridge of her nose. "I shouldn't have stayed away so long."

Jules sat up. "There was nothing you could have done," she said. "No one was traveling. You lost a ton of business, too."

Dad sneezed into his elbow, knocking the cards over as he turned. Mateo groaned. After wiping his nose with a handkerchief, Dad turned to Sylvia. "She's right, you know? There's nothing you could have done. Even if you had been here the whole time."

Sylvia bent over her laptop again. "Still . . ." she said.

Lu and Raquel sat in the last empty seats at the table and helped Mateo pick up the scattered cards. Raquel took two and balanced them against each other so they made a small, wobbly tent. Then she balanced two more alongside it. But when she tried to lay a fifth card across the two towers, the whole thing collapsed.

"Next time, build the bases closer together," Mateo advised. "It's stronger that way."

Lately, this new family they were supposed to be building felt a little like that card tower. Fragile. But no one had told them how to stack the cards the right way. They were supposed to just *know*.

As Mateo began again, Tía Enriqueta appeared in the doorway. Her hair was pulled back in a gold barrette, and she was wearing the same necklace that she had the other night—the one with the garnets. She touched it before speaking.

"Bueno. You're back," she said.

Everyone stopped to listen, but she spoke only to Jules and Sylvia, turning from one to the other.

"I am sorry I kept our troubles from you," she started. "I thought the situation would improve, and I didn't want to worry you."

"I would have come—" Sylvia said, standing.

Tía Enriqueta shook her head. "You and Julieta have been busy with your own lives." Sylvia's eyes dropped to the floor.

"The truth is, I don't know what will happen to the

ranch," Tía Enriqueta went on. "But I want you to have a piece of it."

"A piece?" Jules asked.

"It's in the study," Tía Enriqueta replied. "Raquel, I believe you are staying in there. May we go inside?"

Raquel hesitated, wishing she hadn't left a pile of Corn Chex crumbs on the desktop. But she couldn't exactly refuse. "Sí," she agreed. "Of course."

Tía Enriqueta turned and started toward the study. When only Sylvia and Jules followed, she waved for the rest of them to come, too. "Por favor," she said. "*All* of you."

Lu waited for Dad to slide his chair away from the table before she stood. She nudged Raquel's shoulder on their way down the hall. "It's a good sign, don't you think?" she said. "That she wants *all* of us there?"

"Mmm," Raquel murmured uncertainly, trying to work out what the surprise might be. A part of the ranch? Maybe that old scrapbook, Raquel guessed, grateful she had returned it to its shelf.

But when Tía Enriqueta went straight for the desk, Raquel's chest tightened.

Tía Enriqueta sat on the chair, frowned at the cereal crumbs, and reached for the middle drawer. She paused and lifted her eyes. They sparkled with a playfulness Raquel had never seen there before. "I haven't shown this to anyone in years," she said. *"Decades."*

"Oh no," Lu whimpered, finally understanding what was happening. She stumbled back into the hall as Tía Enriqueta took a tiny key from her pocket and opened the hidden drawer.

"You all right, mija?" Dad whispered.

"Fine," Lu answered, her face pale.

Tía Enriqueta's smile twisted into a worried line of confusion. "This is where I always kept it," she murmured.

Maybe it was only a coincidence, Raquel told herself, trying to slow her heartbeat. Maybe there was something *else* in that drawer. Who would give away their old diary as a gift, anyway?

"Kept what?" Jules asked. "What are you looking for?"

Tía Enriqueta reached farther back. "A . . . sort of . . . book," she said. "It should be here."

Sylvia moved closer to her aunt and knelt to peer into

the desk. "May I help? Maybe it got pushed to the back by one of the guests. Or maybe you moved it and forgot?"

Raquel wiped her clammy palms on her shorts. She stepped toward them. She wasn't sure *how* she was going to explain what the diary was doing under a pillow on her bed. But she couldn't let them keep searching for something that wasn't there. More importantly, the blurry outline of a new idea—an idea that involved the diary—had begun to take shape in her mind. She hadn't planned to share it yet. But things don't always go as planned.

"What did it look like?" Sylvia continued. "Raquel, you didn't happen to notice a book in here, did you?"

"Actually, I—" Raquel started, her voice too squeaky for anyone to hear.

Anyone except Lu, who pinched her elbow.

"Ow!" Raquel said, rubbing her arm. "What was that for?"

Lu pulled her back to the doorway. "You can't tell them you took it," she said. "Not now."

19

Sooner or later they'd give up and search somewhere else. They had to. When they did, she and Raquel would be able to figure out where to put the diary so that no one would ever know Raquel had taken it in the first place. How could Raquel even *consider* telling them she had it? Especially now, when Tía Enriqueta finally seemed to be warming up to them. Sure, it was only a degree or two warmer, but *still*.

Maybe Jules had been right. Maybe Kel *was* trying to sabotage the wedding. Lucinda shuddered, surprised she had allowed the thought to drift into her mind. Raquel had gotten carried away following her next big story, that was all. And just like always, it had led them into a terrible mess. They could still fix it, though. The first step was to get everyone out of the study before they stumbled on something they shouldn't.

"Umm... What about what Sylvia said?" she asked, trying to swallow the shake in her voice. "Could it be somewhere else? Like maybe some other room?"

Tía Enriqueta turned her head sharply. Lucinda flinched. "No. This is where it has been for sixty years. I have never moved it."

Sylvia stood. "Well, this drawer is empty." She put her hands on her hips and gazed around the room, looking for likely hiding places. Lucinda edged her way toward the bed, trying to ignore Raquel's insistent stare.

"Maybe it got put on one of the bookshelves by mistake?" Jules suggested. "When the room was being cleaned between guests?"

Sylvia clapped her hands together. "That's a good idea, mija. Let's see if we can find it on the shelves. Tía, what color is it?"

Tía Enriqueta slouched on the desk chair, dazed and weary.

"Tía?" Sylvia said again.

Lucinda could have answered for her. *Green with little white flowers.*

"Verde," Tía Enriqueta said. "Con floritas blancas."

Dad nodded and started searching the top shelf of the bookcase nearest the window. Sylvia and Jules took the shelves below.

Once their backs were turned, Lucinda grabbed Raquel by the elbow and led her to the shelves on the opposite wall. "Come on," she said. "Let's look over here."

They crouched, half hidden by the bed. "I have to tell them," Raquel whispered. She looked at Tía Enriqueta, who still sat behind the desk, twisting her garnet cross. "She seems really upset."

"No!" Too loud. Jules turned, eyebrows scrunched. "No ... don't ... go so fast. You might damage the books," Lucinda fumbled.

Once Jules turned away, she whispered, "Just a few more minutes, Kel. *Please.*" She pulled a book off the bottom shelf, pretended to look behind it for the diary she knew wasn't there, then put it back. "They'll give up and look somewhere else. Then we can figure out what to do."

Raquel opened her mouth—probably to argue again. But before she could, Dad, still combing through the shelves across the room, said, "Is there a guest log? A list of everyone who has stayed in this room? Maybe we can call and see if they remember seeing it."

Lucinda jumped to her feet. "Great idea."

Sylvia rubbed her temples and looked hopelessly at the stack of books she and Jules had already taken down, none of them the diary. "It's worth a shot, I guess."

Lucinda was already halfway to the door. "I'll go ask Cousin Elena."

She should never have left Raquel's side.

"Wait," Raquel said, rising slowly off the hardwood floor.

Jules froze. Sylvia looked up from the cover of an encyclopedia volume she was dusting with the sleeve of her blouse. Tía Enriqueta lifted her chin in Raquel's direction.

"Ra*quel* . . ." Lucinda whined one last time, knowing

she had already lost. Like when she fell at the beginning of a figure skating performance, but had to struggle through to the finish anyway.

Trust me, Raquel mouthed.

Sylvia shelved the encyclopedia and began walking slowly toward Raquel. When she reached her, she brushed back a strand of dark brown hair that had fallen across Raquel's eyes. "What is it?"

Raquel took a deep breath. She looked down at the floor, then up at Sylvia. Watching from the doorway, Lucinda laced her fingers into knots, wishing there was something she could do to stop this. Like scream. Or throw her shoe out the window. But she had never been that kind of daring.

"Don't get the guest log," Raquel said finally. "You don't have to. I know where the diary is."

Now Dad moved toward her, too. "Raquel?" But everyone else became very still as Raquel went to the bed and, one by one, moved aside the neatly stacked pillows. Underneath them was the treasure that everyone had been hunting for.

Raquel clung to the diary with both hands. She carried it to Tía Enriqueta, who stared at her for a moment before snatching the book and opening it frantically. She turned to the back and stopped to run her finger over one of the last pages. Then she lifted her hand and snapped.

"¿Un cuchillo? ¿Algo? Por favor."

Jules darted out of the room. She returned, not with a knife, but with the pair of craft scissors she'd packed even though Sylvia had told her not to. "Will these work?"

Tía Enriqueta reached out her hand. "Dámelas." Jules gave her the scissors, and she used them to cut a thin strip off the edge of the back page, which, Lucinda realized, was really two pages pasted together. Tía Enriqueta slid a finger between them.

Finally, her shoulders relaxed as she pulled out a square of pale blue stationery, folded tight.

"It's the recipe," she said, then corrected herself. "My *grandfather's* recipe. For the obleas." She pressed her lips together as she studied the paper in her palm. "I wanted you to have it, but now . . ." She turned to Raquel. "Why would you do this?"

"I—" Raquel started.

Jules cut her off. "You were trying to ruin the wedding!" she yelled, pointing. "I knew we couldn't trust you."

Raquel shook her head so hard her hair fell back into her face. She didn't try to brush it away. "No," she insisted. "That's not it. Let me explain. I was trying to help—"

"Ha!" Jules scoffed. "As if we'd believe that? After everything you've done? After you didn't even want to be here in the first place?"

"Jules, please," Lucinda begged. "It's not like that. Kel was . . . I mean . . ." She realized she still didn't know *what* Raquel was trying to do. "She had a plan."

Jules rolled her eyes. "Of course you're taking *her* side. You always take her side."

They were supposed to be on the same side. They were supposed to be a team.

"Girls, that's enough," Sylvia said. She put her hand on Tía Enriqueta's shoulder. "I'm sure there is some explanation for this. Would all of you please give Raquel and me a few minutes to talk?"

Jules stomped off, and Tía Enriqueta followed without

another word, taking the diary with her. Dad stood in front of Raquel and raised an eyebrow, silently asking if she was all right, the way he used to do before leaving them at birthday parties or on the first day of school.

Raquel nodded.

"Bueno," he said.

Lucinda felt glued to the floor. She couldn't leave. She had to explain to Sylvia that even though this *was* Raquel's fault, it also wasn't, or at least it wasn't her fault in the way that it probably seemed. But Dad was leading her out the door. "Let's go," he said. "It'll be fine."

20

Lucinda shut the door behind her. The room was almost empty now and suddenly quiet. Yet it still felt crowded with all their misunderstandings.

Raquel stared out the window and the odd mirror beside it, thinking again about the house of cards they'd been building only a little while earlier and how easily it had blown down. She could leave the pieces scattered, or she could begin again, one card at a time. She snuck a glance at Sylvia, who had taken Tía Enriqueta's place behind the desk and was absently twisting a paper clip.

Maybe she was figuring out what to say. Maybe she was waiting for Raquel to go first. Raquel decided that all she wanted right then was for Sylvia to know the truth.

She imagined herself picking up a card and balancing it on its edge. Slowly. Carefully. "I wasn't trying to sabotage the wedding," she said.

In her mind, she picked up another card and leaned it gingerly against the first. "I was trying to help."

Sylvia dropped the paper clip and studied Raquel's face, saying nothing.

Raquel wished she had her notebook—or anything—to hold on to. Instead, she clenched her hands into fists. She waited for the cards to fall.

They didn't.

Sylvia sighed and said simply, "I know."

Raquel had been prepared to explain, prepared to defend herself. She was not prepared for this. She opened her mouth, then closed it again. She wrinkled her nose. "You *know*?"

Sylvia gestured toward the bed, inviting Raquel to sit. She must have read Raquel's mind. Because now that she had told Sylvia the truth—or at least the beginning of the truth—Raquel realized that what she most wanted was to sit. To catch her breath and to stop trying to think three thoughts ahead. She collapsed on the quilt and hugged one of the pillows to her chest the way Lucinda had done.

Sylvia stood and walked toward the bookcase, humming to herself. She started replacing the volumes that Jules and Dad had left in a stack on the rug. "I know you didn't want to come here," she said.

Raquel stiffened. She was wrong. Sylvia *didn't* understand. "No, that's *not* it, I just . . ." She wanted to say that she wasn't against the marriage, and it wasn't even that she didn't want to be at the wedding. But it was getting harder and harder to figure out where she fit anymore, to hold on to the things she cared most about. Nothing felt normal, and no one could say whether it ever would again. No one could tell her how much *more* would change.

But before she could attempt to arrange it all into words that made sense, Sylvia said, "Wait. That came out wrong. Let me try again." She closed her eyes and inhaled deeply before opening them. "I know that coming to

Mexico would not have been your *first* choice. And maybe you wouldn't have even chosen for your dad and me to be together if it was up to you. But you're here anyway. You did that for us."

Raquel looked down at her socks, bright white against the rich browns of the floor. "I kinda did it so that Lu would owe me a favor," she admitted. "That wasn't the *only* reason, though," she added quickly.

Even though it wasn't easy to be away from home, she had wanted Dad and Sylvia to be happy. Just like she wanted the five of them to have memories that were part of the same story instead of pages pulled from separate books.

"Well, the point is, you came." Sylvia laughed. "I know how much you love your family. I know I'm lucky to be part of it."

Sylvia still hadn't asked about the diary. It was a detail Raquel thought she would remember for a long time, even if she didn't write it down. She decided that if Sylvia could trust her, then she could trust Sylvia to listen as she tried to explain.

"I didn't mean to steal the diary—I didn't even know it existed until I found it," she began. "And I know I should have left it alone. But then I thought that if I could understand Tía Enriqueta—sort of get inside her head—maybe I would know how to make her . . . *like* us. And then . . ."

She stopped herself before she went any further. What she almost said was that then she had gotten swept away by the mystery of the recipe. It had been so long since she had found a story she could put together like a puzzle whose picture wouldn't be revealed until she had found every piece. But that would be too many surprises for one afternoon. And anyway, she wasn't completely sure yet that her suspicions about the recipe—and exactly whom it was stolen from—were correct.

Sylvia crossed the room and sat next to Raquel on the bed.

"It isn't your job to make Tía Enriqueta like you," she said. "She should see how much *I* love you—how much we all love one another. If she doesn't, then she's the one who needs to make an adjustment, not you."

She paused, running her finger over a small tear in the

quilt. "I would like her to be at the wedding, but that's her choice to make, just like it was yours."

Raquel wasn't ready to lean her head on Sylvia's shoulder yet, like she would have if it had been Mom sitting there. She knew Sylvia would have let her, though, and that was enough.

"Thanks," Raquel said.

Sylvia ruffled her hair. "I'm just sorry I let that recipe slip through my hands! You didn't happen to copy it down in one of your notebooks, did you?"

Raquel groaned. She almost *never* missed important details, yet somehow she had gotten so distracted by the words on the diary's pages that she failed to see what was between them. "I didn't notice it was there!" she confessed.

"Oh well," Sylvia said. "Maybe some other time. I'll leave you alone. Come out when you're ready."

She got off the bed and spun slowly around, looking at the room as if she wanted to memorize it. Then she left.

21

Lucinda stood in the hall outside Jules's door, wondering whether she should knock. A part of her wanted to. The part that was always in a hurry to smooth over raw edges. But another part felt bruised that Jules hadn't stuck up for Raquel. Worse, that she'd been the first one to accuse her.

So instead of knocking, Lucinda decided to follow Dad into the living room.

He was in front of the fireplace, looking at family pictures on the mantel. Lucinda stood beside him, and he rubbed her shoulders as if he could sense how being pulled in two directions for so long had left them aching.

Then he took down a silver frame with a picture of Sylvia and Jules inside. They were riding horses on the ranch. Jules was seven or eight, maybe, and a breeze was blowing her hair off her shoulders. It felt strange to think that none of them could have known then that, one day, they would all end up here together. Dad set the picture back down. Lucinda could tell he was listening for any sounds that might come out of the study. She was, too.

"What do you think they're talking about?" she asked.

Dad lifted his eyes toward the ceiling and shoved his hands deep into his pockets. "¿Quién sabe?" he said finally. "Let's sit."

They went to the table where Mateo, Sarita, and Alejandra were quietly playing lotería. Mateo slid a tabla across the table to each of them. He pulled the next card. *El paraguas.*

"I have it!" Lucinda took a dried pinto bean from the bowl at the center of the table and placed it on the umbrella illustration at the bottom corner of her tabla. The next card Mateo drew was *La bandera*.

Alejandra looked up from her tabla and glanced quickly in the direction of the study. The cousins must have heard everything.

Finally, the footsteps they'd all been listening for padded softly down the hall. Dad stood as Sylvia walked into the room. He let a handful of beans fall to the table. "¿Qué pasó?"

"We had a good talk," Sylvia answered. "I know her heart was in the right place."

"Should I go in to see her?"

Sylvia shook her head. "I think she needs a few minutes. And Juliette?"

"In her room."

Sylvia nodded. "Let's give her some time, too," she said. "And then, maybe tomorrow, once we've all had a chance to clear our heads, we can talk. *Again*."

Lucinda couldn't wait until tomorrow. For one thing, she wouldn't be able to sleep not knowing whether Jules was still angry, not knowing what Raquel and Sylvia had discussed, just . . . *not knowing*. She got up and ran down the hall, stopping at the door to the old study.

It was still closed. She put her ear against it and strained to listen for clues about what was happening inside—Raquel crunching on Corn Chex or scribbling in her notebook. But she heard nothing. She knocked.

There was no answer.

She knocked again, this time cracking the door open as she did so. "Kel?" she said. It wasn't like Raquel to ignore her, especially when Lucinda made it clear she wasn't going to go away.

When there was still no answer, she pushed the door open and stepped inside.

The room was silent, as tidy as when they first arrived. All the books had been returned to their shelves, and the desk had been put back to order. The only sign that Raquel had ever been there was her duffel bag on the floor by the bed.

"Are you in here?" Lucinda asked, knowing she wasn't. Her fingers trembled as she took her phone from her pocket and texted Raquel.

Where are you?

A moment later, she heard a muffled buzz coming from inside the desk. Lucinda opened the center drawer. *Perfect.* Raquel had left her phone behind, and Lucinda knew it wasn't an accident.

She took a deep, shaky breath and tried to stay calm. But panic was already rising, so that when someone tapped her shoulder, she jumped.

"Sorry for scaring you," Alejandra said. "We just wanted to find out what was going on, and Julieta won't let us in." Mateo and Sarita stood at either side of her.

"She's not here," Lucinda said. She walked over to the closet and flung open its door. Empty except for some of Raquel's clothes. Next, she tried under the bed.

"What do you mean?" Sarita asked.

"She's not here," Lucinda repeated. "My sister. But that doesn't make any sense. We would have heard her come down the hallway if she left the room."

Sarita, Mateo, and Alejandra looked at one another.

"Maybe not," Mateo said.

He walked toward the full-length mirror on the wall

beside the window. He ran his fingers along the mirror's edge. Lucinda heard a small pop, and the mirror swung open on a hinge, revealing a door behind it.

"They built it a long time ago,' Mateo said. "During the revolution. In case anyone ever needed to escape."

Another secret door, just like Jules had told them. Of course Raquel would have found it. Lucinda turned the knob and shoved the door open with her shoulder. She poked her head outside. The evening's first crickets had begun to chirp.

"We'll go with you," Sarita said.

Lucinda leaned back into the room. "¿De veras?" she asked with a mix of surprise and relief. She would have gone looking on her own if she had to, but it would be easier with someone who knew the ranch. Still, she couldn't help asking, "Why?"

"You're family," Sarita said with a shrug. "We should hurry, though. It's getting dark."

"Maybe she's not far," Mateo suggested. "Maybe she's only on the patio."

Lucinda wished that were true. But if Raquel wanted to

be alone, she wouldn't have chosen a spot where the family was so likely to find her. "I don't think so," she said.

"We could check the goat pen," Alejandra said.

That's where *Lucinda* might have gone—not that the goats could *ever* replace Crybaby—but Raquel wasn't the type to talk to animals when she needed to clear her mind.

Lucinda closed her eyes and pictured Raquel, remembering the last time she had run off.

"The apple orchard."

Standing below the tree house, they could see a candle's dim light glowing through the windows.

"Kel?" Lucinda called up, shining the flashlight Alejandra had snuck from a kitchen cupboard. "Is that you?"

"What are you doing here?" a voice called back. Then Raquel leaned her head out the window. She blinked into the light and noticed Sarita, Alejandra, and Mateo standing behind Lucinda. "What are *all* of you doing here?"

Lucinda's fear cooled to relief, but was quickly heating up again to annoyance. "Trying to find *you*, obviously," she said. "You didn't tell anyone you were leaving and you didn't take your phone with you. You scared me."

A corner of Raquel's mouth turned down. "Sorry. Hold on."

They waited at the base of the tree house while Raquel clambered down the ladder. "I was going to come right back," she said. "I just needed to figure something out."

"Figure what out?" Lucinda asked.

"How to make sure Jules and Sylvia can bring home a piece of the ranch," she said, eyes glittering. "I'm glad you're all here because I'll need your help."

22

Raquel stretched her toes, then kicked off the quilt. Waking up early had always been easy for her, especially when she had a plan to look forward to. And for the first time in what felt like months, she had a good one. A plan that had nothing to do with the newspaper but everything to do with telling a new story. A family story.

Much harder than opening her eyes, though, was working up the courage to get out of bed and creep down the hall to the kitchen, where she knew Cousin Elena was probably making breakfast. But if her plan had any chance of working, she couldn't put it off any longer.

As predicted, Elena was standing at the sink, rinsing nopales. What Raquel did not predict was that Mateo, Alejandra, and Sarita—and even Lucinda, whom she usually had to drag out of bed—would be there, too.

"They've all been waiting for you," Elena said, raising an eyebrow. "But they won't tell me what for."

Raquel had hoped to find Elena alone so that she could apologize for taking the diary. She wasn't sure what Elena had overheard the evening before, or, worse, what Tía Enriqueta had told her. But before Raquel could begin the speech she had rehearsed late into the night, and for at least a half hour that morning, Elena turned off the faucet.

"And I don't suppose you're going to tell me, either," she said with a wink. She didn't seem angry or suspicious. Or even like she was waiting for an explanation. She pulled two paper towels from the roll on the counter and patted the cactus dry.

"Well, it's sort of a surprise," Raquel said, confidence

returning. "Can we borrow the kitchen for the morning? Or maybe...all day?" She wasn't sure how long this would take. She had never done it, after all.

Elena looked around at the five of them, leaning over the kitchen island. "Do I have a choice?" She laughed and turned back to Raquel. "Your parents are out on a walk. Come find me if you need anything. I'll be in the back, helping Luis with the plumbing." Then she pointed to a pastry box near the stove. "There's pan dulce for breakfast."

"¡Por fin!" Sarita burst out, and dove for the box. While Sarita arranged the pastries on a plate, Elena dropped the nopales into plastic bags and stored them in the refrigerator.

"Good luck, mija," she said, patting Raquel on the shoulder on her way out of the kitchen.

Sarita set the plate of pan dulce in the middle of the island.

"So, what are we going to do?" Mateo asked, reaching for a flaky oreja.

Raquel took a breath. This might turn out to be one

more failure, but it was worth trying. "Obleas," she said.

"The candy?" Lucinda asked with a yawn.

"For Sylvia," Raquel said. "She wanted them for the wedding, and she's always saying they remind her of being here. I thought that if we could figure out the recipe, then whatever happens . . ." She stopped herself, glancing at Mateo and Sarita and Alejandra. If the family lost the ranch, they'd lose their home. No recipe, no matter how sweet, could replace that. "Well, whatever happens, we'd have the recipe to remember the first time we were here together." And they could all hope it wouldn't be the last.

No one answered at first. Raquel wondered if she had gone too far. Maybe it wasn't really *her* family recipe, after all. Maybe they didn't want to share it.

"Abuela always makes the obleas," Sarita said after a while. "But we've seen her do it."

"And we know the ingredients," Alejandra added. "The wafers are easy, only flour and water."

Mateo pulled a foldable step stool from where it was stored between the stove and refrigerator. He climbed on top to reach one of the highest cupboards. "And," he said, opening it, "we know where she keeps *this*." He took out a kitchen tool that looked a little like a waffle maker, only smaller, and held it up like a trophy.

So that's *where Sylvia got her love for kitchen gadgets*, Raquel thought.

Sarita continued. "And for the cajeta, we need sugar and—"

"Goat's milk!" Alejandra finished the sentence.

It was almost like being at the center of a newspaper club meeting again, ideas flying, everyone working together to create something better than what they could have made on their own.

Mateo climbed down from the stepladder and opened another cupboard. Inside was a neat stack of forest-green aprons. Mateo took out five of them and tossed one to Raquel. *Flor de Manzana* was embroidered across the chest in white letters. In place of the *o* was an apple blossom.

"The milk has to be fresh," Sarita went on. "That's what Abuela always says. I'll go and milk Luna."

"I'll help!" Lu said. "I didn't get a chance yesterday." She tightened the sweatshirt she always wore tied around her waist. Even though it was summer and even though the nearest ice rink was more than a hundred miles away. (Raquel had checked before they left to convince Lu *not* to pack her skates.)

"Hold on a sec?" Raquel had another job for her sister. The milk wasn't the only ingredient they still needed.

"Yeah?" Lu turned.

Raquel almost tripped on one last pebble of doubt. If Lu and Jules didn't make up, then maybe Lu wouldn't have any reason to stay in Lockeford once summer was over. Maybe she would come home to Los Angeles.

But Raquel knew that without Jules, the recipe couldn't be complete. She kicked the doubt away and slipped the apron over her head.

"Could you get Jules?" she asked, trying to make it sound as if it were no big deal, even though she knew that it was.

Lu bit her bottom lip. "I think she still needs some space," she said. "She'll come out when she's ready."

Mateo scooped some flour into a glass bowl. Alejandra poured water over it.

"Tell her we need her," Raquel insisted.

"Can't someone else do it?"

"Please, Lu?" Raquel said. "She trusts you."

23

It was just like Raquel to leave Lucinda stuck with the hardest part of one of her plans. Lucinda would have preferred to measure the flour. Or learn how to use that kitchen contraption Mateo found. Or milk the goats. Or even wipe down the goats' udders. Anything that wasn't confronting Jules, who was probably still as angry as she had been the night before. Still as unwilling to listen.

But Raquel was right. This plan—their best one yet, without secrets, without schemes—wouldn't work without Jules. It wasn't only that they needed her help with the recipe. Maybe the recipe wasn't even the point. Maybe it was like Lucinda had tried to explain to Raquel back in Lockeford, that being a team was about more than playing the same game. It was about trying and failing and figuring things out. Together.

Raquel would keep them organized. She would make sure they didn't lose sight of their goal—or the time. Jules could bring her creativity. The adventurous way she put different pieces together, whether cooking ingredients or craft supplies, to make something new. If she wanted to, she could help stitch Lucinda and Raquel into this new family.

Rounding the corner into the hall, Lucinda wondered what she could bring when all she ever seemed to do was ping-pong nervously between Raquel and Jules.

Then again, maybe that was it. Maybe her job, at least for now, *was* to stand between them, to help them see the best in each other until they knew how to do it on their own. She could turn them into a team instead of individual players.

The sting Lucinda had felt last night had mostly dulled.

She could ignore what was left, but ignoring it wouldn't make it go away. For that, she had to knock on Jules's door.

Still, she hesitated. She tried to send Jules a silent message the way she sometimes did with Raquel, even though it mostly never worked. *Please come out,* she thought. *And when you do, please let everything be back to normal.*

Then Lucinda heard something. Not a reply, but a dull thudding. She pressed her ear against the door and strained to listen. It was Jules, pacing from one end of the room to the other, like a cat with too much nervous energy.

So, Jules was worried, too. Maybe she was even hoping someone would come find her. Finally, Lucinda raised her hand to knock, but stopped herself yet again, lowering her fist to her side. She had a better idea.

She backed away from the door and tiptoed to her room. She walked past the sun-soaked window seat and the brightly painted writing desk and went straight for the closet. She opened it and pushed aside the clothes and spare blankets. Behind them was the secret passage that led to Jules's room.

Lucinda crouched and reached her hand inside to judge how cramped it would be. She jerked her arm back when the first thing she touched was a cobweb.

"*Yech!*" she whispered, shaking it off. If Raquel had been there, she'd give her a push. "Just *go*, Lu," she'd say. (And of course she'd be prepared with some very important reason *she* had to stay behind while Lucinda dove into the spider pit alone.)

But since Raquel wasn't there, Lucinda would have to do the pushing herself.

She borrowed some advice from her coach. "Don't overthink it," she murmured. "You know what to do."

She put her head down and crawled in.

The dark didn't last long, and at the other side of it, Lucinda found herself in what looked like a replica of her own closet. In this version, Jules's running shoes, her warm-up jacket, and the bag of scrap fabric she had packed in case they needed it for wedding decorations lay scattered on the floor.

Light shone through the gap below the closet door. Peering out, Lucinda thought she could see Jules's socks on the rug. She eased herself a little farther into the closet, unsure what to do next. Was she supposed to knock? She continued inching forward, but in the dim light, she didn't notice Jules's suitcase until she crashed into it. It toppled forward with a bang against the door.

Lucinda cringed as Jules's feet came rushing toward the closet.

"H-hello?" she said.

Lucinda reached over the suitcase and pushed the door open. She looked up at Jules, who held her jump rope over her head like a whip, ready to strike.

"Don't!" Lucinda cried, throwing her hands over her face. "It's just me!"

Jules exhaled as she dropped her arm. "Why'd you sneak up on me like that?" she said. "I almost *fainted*." Her mouth began to twitch. For one terrible moment, Lucinda thought Jules was about to cry. Instead, she started laughing. It burst out like a bark that mellowed into a long, uncontrollable cackle, until Jules actually *did* start crying.

At least it was the good kind.

"Were you going to attack me with the...j-jump rope?" Lucinda had started laughing, too, and could hardly get the word out. She stood, shaking off one of Jules's socks that had somehow ended up attached to her shoulder.

"I was scared, and it was the first thing I could find!" Jules said. She tossed the jump rope onto her bed. Her cheeks were still red, but her breathing had begun to slow. "What are you doing here, anyway?"

Lucinda looked around the room. Unlike hers, it didn't have a window seat, but on one wall, there was a mural of hummingbirds and butterflies flitting around a hibiscus tree that made the room feel just as bright and open.

"You're not going to stay in here all day, are you?" Lucinda asked. Her gaze drifted to the end table near Jules's bed and the plate on top of it, empty except for a few rainbow sprinkles. Elena must have brought her a galleta from the pastry box. Maybe Jules *wasn't* planning to leave the room. She would have to convince her. "Come on. We need your help with something in the kitchen."

"Help with what?" Jules plopped, cross-legged, on the bed.

"It's a surprise that Raquel came up with. For your mom," Lucinda explained. "But don't worry. It doesn't involve any garlic powder, I promise."

She forced a smile, *wanting* to be able to joke about the things that happened during their first weeks together in Lockeford, but worried it was still too soon.

"No thanks," Jules said. "I was getting ready to go out for a run." She turned her head to the window, which, like Lucinda's, looked out over the patio. "Anyway, Raquel probably doesn't want me there."

"Raquel's the one who told me to come get you."

Jules snapped her head back around. "She *did*?" Her shoulders dropped. "But what about you?" she asked, not looking at Lucinda. "Are you sure *you* want me there? Mom told me what happened. I should have known Raquel didn't steal the diary. I wish I hadn't said all those things."

Lucinda sat next to her. She kicked her legs against the light blue bedspread. She was about to tell Jules not to worry about it. That it didn't matter.

Except it *did* matter. And if they were going to be sisters, or even something like sisters, it was worth saying so. "I wish you hadn't, either," she said. "But I get that you were scared. And I know we haven't always made it easy for you to trust us. Kel gets that, too. Maybe we can try again . . . *again*?"

Jules smiled, and this time it didn't crumble. "Deal. So what's the surprise?"

24

Sarita returned, carrying the heavy milk pail, and Mateo
ran over to help her with the door.

"Set it on the counter," Raquel said as Alejandra ladled
the last of the thin wafer batter onto the iron. "We're
almost finished with these." The rhythm now familiar to
her, Raquel pressed the top half of the iron down, spread-
ing the puddle of batter into a thin pancake. Thirty
seconds later, when steam started to escape the sides and
the air around them began to smell like warm toast, she
lifted it open again. Alejandra took a spatula and

carefully lifted the cooked wafer off the iron and moved it over to a tray with the rest.

"That's all," Alejandra said, wiping her hands on her apron. "Now we let them cool."

Raquel picked up one of the warm wafers, blob-shaped like an ink spot when one of her pens broke, and scowled at it. "We must have done something wrong," she said, frustrated she hadn't noticed it sooner. "The ones I saw in the pictures were perfectly round. Are these even going to work?"

Already she began calculating whether there were enough ingredients, enough time—enough team spirit— to start again with a new batch.

"They're never perfect to start." The voice came from just outside the kitchen. A moment later, Jules walked in, Lu right behind her.

"Tía Enriqueta always fixes them up later," Jules continued. "Mateo, do you remember where she keeps the kitchen shears?"

"Shears?"

"Like scissors," she explained. "But for food?"

"I think I know," Alejandra said.

While Alejandra pulled open a drawer and began to rummage through it, Raquel grabbed the one apron that was still folded on the counter. She tossed it to Jules.

"You're right on time," Raquel said. "I never would have figured that out on my own."

Jules slipped the apron over her head and tied it around her waist. "Of course you would have," she replied. "But thanks for saying so. And, Kel?" She fidgeted with the ends of the apron strings. "I'm sorry for what I said, and—"

"I know," Raquel said, remembering her conversation with Sylvia and what a relief it was, sometimes, when you didn't have to explain. "Anyway, we better hurry. Dad and Sylvia could come back any minute now, and I want this to be a surprise."

Alejandra slammed the drawer closed and spun around. "Aha!" she said, holding up the shears.

Jules took them from her. "Vamos," she said, picking up one of the wafers.

"So, you're just going to *cut* it?" Lu asked. "Like paper or something?"

"Mm-hmm." Jules nodded. Then she carefully trimmed off the uneven edges of the wafer until it was perfectly smooth and round.

Raquel picked up one of the scraps that had fallen to the counter and set it on her tongue. She chewed and swallowed. The wafers didn't just cut like paper. They tasted like it, too. "You guys, we *definitely* did something wrong." This thin, bland cracker could not be what Sylvia was remembering every time she told them about the obleas. It couldn't be the secret that Tía Enriqueta kept hidden in her diary for so many years.

Mateo started to giggle, then Jules did, too. "Don't worry," she said. "They'll taste a *lot* better with the cajeta inside."

They got to work. Lu and Raquel poured the goat's milk into a heavy pot that Sarita set over the stove. Then Alejandra stirred in some sugar after she, Mateo, and Jules argued over how much Tía Enriqueta usually added. In the end they compromised, scooping in a little less than what Mateo thought was right and a little more than Jules did.

"I feel like we're in one of Mom's videos," Lucinda said, not bothering to lower her voice.

"If she made a video that was all outtakes and bloopers, then yeah," Raquel agreed. "I could see that."

"Very funny," Jules said. "Let's see who's laughing when it's finished."

Sarita dropped a vanilla pod into the pot. "Now we wait for it to bubble," she said.

Raquel stood back as they all watched the pot. "What if . . . ?" she said, mostly to herself.

"Huh?" Jules looked up at her.

Raquel shook her head. "Nothing really, I was just thinking . . ." she began. "Remember how you told us Tía Enriqueta had a secret ingredient? Something that made it better than the candy company's version?"

Jules nodded.

"Well, what if we added our own secret ingredients?"

Jules turned down the flame on the burner. "Like what?"

Raquel wasn't sure yet. She just knew that she wanted the cajeta to taste like home, even if that meant something different than what it used to mean.

"What about a little cinnamon?" Lucinda suggested.

"Like what Elena puts in the hot chocolate every morning."

Sarita darted to the spice rack by the refrigerator and took down a glass jar. She unscrewed the lid and pulled out a cinnamon stick. "Let's try it," she said, tossing the stick into the pot.

"And maybe something from the garden?" Raquel said, thinking about the velvety-sweet smell of the jasmine and the gently burbling fountain.

Lu picked up the kitchen shears. "I saw some rosemary out there. That should work. I'll be right back."

There was still one more flavor Raquel hoped they could stir into the mix. "I wish there was some way to bring in the apples."

Jules drummed her fingers on the counter. Then she turned to her cousins. "Did you make any apple butter last year?"

Mateo grinned. "In the cellar."

While they waited for Lu and Mateo to return, Sarita and Alejandra stirred the milk with a wooden spoon. Jules leaned back against the counter. She pointed at the notebook and pen sticking out of Raquel's shirt pocket.

"Shouldn't you be writing this down?" she asked. "So we can all remember it?"

She was right.

Raquel took out the pen and notebook and turned to a blank page.

They took turns stirring, handing off the wooden spoon each time someone's arm got too tired to keep going.

"It's kind of like a relay, don't you think?" Jules said, taking the spoon from Lucinda.

Except relays usually had a finish line.

"Can we turn the stove up?" Raquel asked. "Won't it cook faster that way?"

Alejandra shielded the knob with her hand. "No! It'll burn if it's too hot. You have to be patient."

Raquel checked the clock again. It had only been forty-five minutes, but it felt like hours. When she glanced back at the milk, she saw that it had begun to turn a light golden brown.

"It's ready!" she said.

"No, it's not!" Jules, Alejandra, and Mateo said in unison.

Lu pulled Raquel away from the stove. "I can't believe I'm saying this," she said. "But maybe you should look at the *Manzanita Mirror* for a little while."

Raquel took out her phone and hoisted herself up onto the counter. She tried to read but could only get through two stories before she was peering over at the pot again.

Now the mixture was darker and thicker.

"I *really* think it's ready now," she insisted.

"Just a . . . little . . . while . . . longer," Jules said in time with the slow rhythm of her stirring. "Trust me."

Raquel groaned.

"Relax," Lu said, laughing. "You're acting the way you do when one of the reporters is late turning in a story."

It was almost the same feeling, Raquel realized. Restless and eager all at once.

Finally, quietly—as if she were afraid to disturb it— Jules announced, "I think it's done. Who wants the first taste?"

"I'd volunteer for that."

It was Dad, standing in the doorway with Sylvia.

25

Maybe the surprise was spoiled, but in some ways this seemed even better than giving the finished obleas to Dad and Sylvia like Raquel had planned. Now they would be part of making them, too. It would be one more memory they could all share. Sometimes Lucinda felt as if she was collecting memories like seashells in a bucket at the beach near Mom's apartment. And that the bucket, which had started out with nothing but sand at the bottom, was slowly beginning to fill.

Raquel took the spoon from Jules and lifted it out of the

pot. Caramel dripped off the end. "I think *Sylvia* should taste it first," she said. "Since she's the expert."

Sylvia rolled up the sleeves of her gauzy white blouse. "Just hand over that spoon," she said. She let a few last drips of gooey caramel ooze back into the pot. Then she brought the spoon to her lips and blew on it. Finally, she closed her eyes and tasted.

The rest of them watched, waiting for her verdict, but Sylvia didn't say anything for several long seconds. It was worse than waiting for the judges' scores during a figure skating competition, Lucinda thought. She shoved both hands into the apron's front pocket to stop herself from biting her fingernails.

When she thought she couldn't stand it any longer, Jules screeched, *"Mom!* Would you just say something already? How is it? Tell us!" She grabbed both of Sylvia's shoulders and shook them.

Sylvia's eyes popped open. A smile lit up her face like a rainbow after a storm. "I didn't think it was possible," she said, looking around at them all. "But this is even better than I remembered. Marcos, you have to try it." She dipped the spoon back into the pot. Dad reached for it, but she pulled her hand away.

"Get your own!" she said, laughing.

Mateo opened the silverware drawer and grabbed a handful of spoons, enough for the rest of them. Dad scooped a bit of cajeta from the side of the pot and nodded as he swallowed. "Now I understand why we had to come all the way down here," he said, going in for another taste.

With everyone crowded around the stove, Lucinda had to duck under Sarita's arm to get to the pot. To her, the cajeta tasted the way she remembered from their first morning at Flor de Manzana, richer than the store-bought caramel sauce they sometimes drizzled over ice cream. Only this time, there was something else. Something more. The sweet-spicy cinnamon that filled her with the warmth of Elena's first welcome to the ranch, the fresh green taste of the rosemary that brought her back to the patio garden, and the faintest hint of apple that would always make her think of the tree house at the center of the moonlit orchard. All the flavors swirled together in a surprising but perfect mix.

Jules took two of the wafers that they had trimmed into circles. She sandwiched a dollop of cajeta between them and handed the finished oblea to Raquel.

"You still haven't had the full experience," she said. "Try this."

Raquel bit down, and the wafers crunched between her teeth. "You were right," she said, covering her mouth with her hand. "The cajeta is everything."

Sylvia helped herself to another spoonful. "I can't believe you pulled this off," she said. "I spent all those years thinking I needed someone else's recipe when I could have made it on my own. Thank you. This means so much to me."

Jules twirled her teaspoon between her fingers. "It was Kel's idea," she said.

"Only at first," Raquel added quickly, putting her arm around Jules's shoulder. "Then we all sort of . . . figured it out."

Jules nudged Sylvia. "I guess putting up with all your kitchen experiments taught me a few things," she teased.

For the first time in days, Lucinda felt like her family

was glued back together with something stickier and sweeter than the cajeta. Which, she realized as she looked into the pot, was dwindling fast.

"We better slow down if we want to have any left for the wedding," she said.

As soon as the words left her mouth, Dad stopped chewing. Sylvia set the wooden spoon down on a dish towel and dabbed the corners of her mouth with a napkin. The kitchen felt suddenly hollow, as if, without realizing what she was doing, Lucinda had broken a magic spell.

Sylvia cleared her throat. "That's something we'd like to talk to you about." She turned to Sarita. "Mija, would you go get your mami for me? We might as well do this all at once."

The minute it took for Sarita to return with Elena was the longest Lucinda could remember. Raquel fidgeted, clicking her pen in and out, in and out.

Finally, Elena walked into the kitchen, Sarita trailing after her. "Do I finally get to find out what the big surprise is?" she asked. She smiled at Dad and Sylvia. "Did your daughters tell you they banished me from the kitchen this morning?"

She looked at the pot and then at the pinched faces surrounding it. Her smile drooped. "¿Qué pasó?" she asked, pulling out a kitchen stool.

Dad took Sylvia's hand and squeezed it.

"Marcos and I have been talking," Sylvia began. "Last night, and some more this morning." She paused, her bottom lip trembling. "And we've decided not to have the wedding here at Flor de Manzana after all."

Lucinda's mouth went dry.

"No!" Jules said, pushing past Mateo to get to Sylvia.

Sylvia pressed her free hand against Jules's check. Then she looked up at the rest of them again. "I know how much time and effort you have put into making this wedding happen," she continued. "But if these are going to be my last memories of the ranch—and I'm going to do everything I can to make sure they're not—I want them to be happy ones. I don't want to keep trying to win Tía Enriqueta over. I don't want you girls to take sides. I just want to remember us here together. Like this."

Lucinda was trying to keep up, but she was still stuck on the first words Sylvia had said. The wedding was off?

How could that be possible after Raquel's latest and best plan had actually come together? After they had done all the hard work of fighting and making up? Like *sisters*? This was the wrong ending.

She turned to Raquel. Maybe Raquel could explain it, or at least explain what they were supposed to do next. But as Lucinda's eyes scanned the group in the kitchen once, and then twice, she realized Raquel wasn't there. With everyone's attention focused on Sylvia, she'd managed to slip away.

26

Raquel had learned more than once over the past strange months that it wasn't always possible to predict what would happen next. That plans could collapse like card towers despite the best preparation. Still, she couldn't help paying attention, couldn't break the habit of thinking two steps ahead to what *might* happen. So when she heard one of the doors to the patio open, then shut, she did a quick mental calculation. With everyone else in the kitchen, waiting to hear Sylvia's announcement, there were only two people it could be: Luis or Tía Enriqueta. And since

Elena said Luis was busy working on the plumbing, Raquel guessed it wasn't him.

She wasn't *planning* to talk to Tía Enriqueta that morning. She wasn't sure she was ready. She needed more time, more research, to confirm her suspicions. But then again, so many things she wasn't ready for had already happened—Dad moving to Lockeford and proposing to Sylvia, for example. You didn't always get to decide what happened and when. But sometimes you got to choose what to do about it.

Raquel had crept only a few steps onto the patio when Tía Enriqueta said, without looking up, "You're making obleas."

It was not a question.

"It was supposed to be a surprise," Raquel replied.

"You think you can surprise me? I would know that smell from miles away." Tía snipped a wilted zinnia bloom off its stem. She opened the scissors again, then sliced through the base of another fading flower. "So it's true? You've stolen the family recipe?"

Raquel took a skittering step backward. She knew Tía

Enriqueta was talking about the recipe in the diary that she never should have opened. It would be easy to say she hadn't stolen the recipe—she hadn't even seen it. That was the truth. But it wasn't *all* of the truth. Her heartbeat sped, and she wondered if this was what Lu felt like the instant before she jumped off the ice.

"It was already stolen," she said. *"From you."*

Tía Enriqueta looked up at Raquel and narrowed her eyes. She took a white handkerchief from her pocket and blotted her forehead with it.

"Sylvia told me you were very smart and . . ."

"Observant?" Raquel guessed. "Determined?"

"Metiche," Tía Enriqueta answered, arching an eyebrow as if daring Raquel to disagree.

Raquel shrugged. She could live with nosy. "What *else* did she say?"

"Plenty." Tía Enriqueta folded her handkerchief and put it back in her pocket. Then she sat on the garden bench and crossed her legs at the ankles. "Maybe I'll tell you more sometime. Pero primero, I want to hear what you think you know about that recipe."

Raquel explained that, when she first read what Tía Enriqueta had written in her diary all those years ago, she thought the family had stolen the recipe from someone else.

But the entry had also made her look at the family pictures in a new way. She noticed that it was always Keta she saw caring for the goats, Keta she saw selling obleas outside the church.

"You must have been the one to collect the milk for the cajeta, too," Raquel said. "But that newspaper story didn't mention you at all. Not even your name. It seemed strange."

Tía Enriqueta tensed. Like Raquel had poked a bruise that was still a little sore.

"I also thought it was strange when Sylvia and Jules said you were the only one who knew the recipe," Raquel continued. "If it was a family tradition, wouldn't you have *shared* it with your family? But it wasn't until you took the recipe out from between those pages that I realized it had been yours all along."

She clicked the pen she was still carrying. Her forehead wrinkled as she tried to piece together the last bits of the puzzle. "But why did it have to be secret? Why didn't your grandfather tell the newspaper the truth?" She imagined what it would feel like to have someone else's name on a story she had written, how Jules would react if someone else took credit for one of her crafts.

Tía Enriqueta didn't answer. She slid over a few inches and nodded at the empty space beside her on the bench. It wasn't exactly a warm invitation, but Raquel decided to accept it anyway. She sat. She waited for the story.

"We had so many goats back then," Tía Enriqueta began. "Not like now. And the *milk*! So much milk. More than we could drink or sell or even feed to the pigs." Her face soured as if she was imagining all those pails of goat's milk and nowhere to put them.

It must have been a little like the mountain of tomatoes that piled up every summer in Lockeford, Raquel thought.

"Pues, we couldn't let it go to waste, of course, so we made cheese. And butter. And yogurt," Tía Enriqueta continued, ticking off dairy products on her fingers. "Even after all that, there was enough milk left over that I asked my amá for a little sugar to make cajeta."

Raquel thought of the beets and how Jules hadn't wanted them to go to waste. "That reminds me of Jules," she said. "Julieta, I mean. She always has ideas about new ways to use things."

Tía Enriqueta smiled. "Sí, she does." Then she returned to her story. "The cajeta was very special, entiendes? We couldn't afford to buy candy at the store then, so the only sweets we had were what I made."

She told how she gave obleas as gifts to friends and how, eventually, the parents of those friends requested big batches for their celebrations. "And paid for them, too," she added, leaning in closer. People from neighboring towns came to the market in Casas Grandes just to sample her obleas.

That's what caught the attention of the man from the candy company. He came in a shiny car to speak with her grandfather about the famous cajeta from Flor de Manzana.

"The ranch was struggling. We needed the money. But who would pay for a little girl's kitchen experiment?" Tía Enriqueta said. "My abuelo told him it was an old family recipe, passed down for generations. He sold him a story, not just a recipe. Y, pues, what could I say?" She raised her arms as if she was really asking. "After we sold the recipe, Abuelo asked me to burn my copy so that no one would ever find out." She twisted the pendant at her neck. "He gave me this to thank me. It has reminded me ever since to protect my family, but I never could burn that recipe."

It wasn't fair. Raquel could not imagine her own family asking for such a sacrifice. Yet she could understand why Tía Enriqueta had made it.

"That's what I was trying to do, too," she said, no longer worried about whether it was her turn to speak. "When I tried to scare Sylvia off, I did it to protect my family. I did it because I was afraid of losing what we had. But I was wrong."

Raquel hesitated. If Lucinda knew what she was about to say, she would have pinched her again to make her stop. "And . . . maybe . . . *you're* wrong, too."

Tía Enriqueta looked toward the house, where Raquel guessed they were still talking about the ruined wedding plans, or maybe wiping the counters and scraping what was left of the cajeta into a jar. "It felt like your father was taking Sylvia and Julieta away from us," she said, so quietly Raquel could barely hear her. "But you're all still here, aren't you?"

She turned to Raquel again. "Do you want to hear what else Sylvia called you?"

Raquel's fist tensed around her pen. "What?" She held her breath.

"Batalladora," Tía Enriqueta said, each of the five syllables like a drumbeat.

Raquel bit her lip, but it wasn't enough to hold back a laugh.

"She called you that, too!"

"Hmm." Tía Enriqueta arched her eyebrow again, but this time, the flicker of a smile lit her face. She put her hands on her knees and began to stand. "Will you come inside with me? I think I need to speak with my family, and I don't want to go alone."

Raquel stood, too. She knew it was time. But she also knew there was more to the story. She took her notebook from her pocket. "Of course. But can I ask you just a few more questions first?"

27

I've been thinking about it for a while now. Please, Mom?

Mom

This a big decision, Lucinda. We'll talk about it when you're home.

The knock was neither gentle nor patient, and the person on the other side didn't bother waiting for a response.

"It's after four o'clock!" Raquel shouted through the

closed door. "You should be dressed by now. We need to finish hanging the papel picado!"

"Says who?" Lucinda answered. She was certain the guests who were already beginning to gather around the fountain wouldn't mind if the patio was missing a few paper banners.

"Says the *whiteboard!*" Raquel said.

"Seriously," Lucinda muttered to herself, sitting at the writing desk and peering at a hand mirror to apply her lip gloss. "Who's the genius who gave her a whiteboard?"

The whiteboard was all anyone had heard about for days. Ever since Dad and Sylvia and Tía Enriqueta had talked and announced that the wedding was back on, the house had been a whirl of activity. There were documents to file at government offices, food to cook, decorations to make. And in the middle of it all, someone—Lucinda suspected it was Elena, even though she refused to confess—had given Raquel a whiteboard and some dry-erase markers.

Major mistake, unless you were the kind of person

who *enjoyed* constant reminders, check-ins, and "just-following-ups."

Raquel had spent hours sketching out a color-coded chart of everything that needed to be done and when—and who was responsible for making it happen. She propped the whiteboard on one of the kitchen counters where no one could miss it. And if, by some miracle, they *did* miss it, Raquel was there to make sure they noticed.

Yet as much as Lucinda wanted the whiteboard to be out of their lives for good, she knew there was no way they could have pulled off this wedding without Raquel's planning.

She did have her limits, though. "Can't someone else hang the papel picado?" she shouted back through the door. "Isn't it more important that we're *dressed*?"

There was a jostling inside her closet and the sound of tumbling boxes. Lucinda looked down just as the closet door popped open and Jules crawled through.

"Actually," she said, "Kel's right. We should be the ones to do it. I want to make sure they don't get tangled."

Jules had stayed up so late finishing the papel picado,

carving intricate shapes into tightly packed stacks of tissue paper, that Sylvia worried she'd be exhausted on the wedding day. The streamers were fragile, so Jules didn't want to hang them that morning when they had arranged the rest of the decorations. A strong breeze might whip them to tatters.

"Can I at least see your dress first?" Lucinda asked.

Jules stood and twirled in a circle.

"It fits!" Lucinda clapped. "And the tie-dye turned out really well."

Raquel's spreadsheets hadn't helped them come to any agreement on bridesmaid's dresses, and they had left for Mexico in such a hurry that there wasn't time to keep shopping back home. Sylvia had said they would find something in Chihuahua, but between Tía Enriqueta's disapproval and the failing ranch and the secret of the diary, they had almost forgotten. Not Raquel, though. And if it hadn't been for her whiteboard—and the two-hour block of shopping time Raquel scheduled on it—they might all be wearing shorts and tank tops to the ceremony.

It was Jules who suggested they split up in the town center and pick out dresses for one another. "It'll be like one last surprise." Then, just as Raquel was about to protest, she added, "Plus, it'll save time. We won't be able to argue."

That settled it. They drew names.

"Talk about a trust exercise," Lucinda had said when Raquel unfolded the slip of paper with her name on it.

"Yes!" Jules cheered when she drew Raquel's name.

That meant Lucinda would buy for Jules. Normally she dreaded big decisions. Worry over who she might disappoint or what would happen if she chose wrong tied her thoughts in impossible knots. And at first, the idea of picking out an outfit for someone else, even if it was Jules—*especially* if it was Jules—gave her a stomachache.

But when she looked inside the shopwindow and saw the white summer dress with short sleeves and a long, billowy skirt, she knew it would be perfect. It reminded her of a blank canvas, and she couldn't wait to see what Jules would turn it into.

Sure enough, the dress was now tie-dyed pink, with a flower made of black satin ribbon sewed at the hip.

"Beets?" Lucinda guessed.

"Leftover jamaica," Jules said. "I hope you don't mind I changed it."

Lucinda shook her head. "That's why I chose it!"

Jules lifted the skirt off the ground. "The best part is, it's long enough that I can wear my running shoes and no one will be able to tell."

Raquel pounded once more on the door before bursting in. She wore a midnight-blue jumpsuit over a cream-colored blouse with tiny white dots. Her wavy brown hair was pulled back into a crown braid Mom had featured in one of her tutorials earlier that summer.

"Do you like it?" Jules asked.

"The pockets are amazing," Raquel said, patting her sides. "They fit *everything*. My phone, my notebook. Pens *and* pencils." She reached into one of the pockets and pulled out a plastic bag of Corn Chex. "And emergency provisions."

"I doubt you'll need them," Jules said. "Mom and Elena

made enough barbacoa to feed the whole state. Not to mention your dad's last-minute carnitas."

"He couldn't exactly say no, after Tía Enriqueta asked if he'd make it for her," Lucinda said. Jules was right, though. There was way too much food to even think about breakfast cereal.

Lucinda zipped up her makeup bag and walked over to the mirror that hung inside the closet door.

Raquel stood behind her right shoulder. "I had to try it on *myself*," she said. "To make sure it would fit you."

Lucinda almost choked picturing Raquel in this dress with its tiers of smoky lavender tulle and shimmering silver beads. "Aw, you really *must* love me," she said.

Raquel shrugged. "Well, we didn't have time for returns or alterations, so."

"I'm still mad you didn't take a picture," Jules said, her face appearing in the mirror on Lucinda's left.

"*Any*way," Raquel said, "I thought that, after the wedding, maybe Jules could turn it into something you could wear for ice skating. When we go home."

The word *home* caught in Raquel's mouth. Lucinda

tried to meet her eyes in the mirror, but Raquel looked away.

"I could definitely do that," Jules said, taking the frilly edge of Lucinda's dress between her fingers. "There's probably enough material here to make a matching headband, too."

She stepped back and considered their reflection. "You know we really don't match. Not even a little bit."

Lucinda tilted her head. "No. But we go together anyway." She took one of Raquel's hands and one of Juliette's. "I still think we should have brought Crybaby, though. Just imagine how adorable he would have looked in a little tuxedo."

She jumped out of the way before Raquel could nudge her with her hip.

"Oh!" Jules said. "Just wait till you see how I dressed Oso and the goats."

28

It was not the normal time to plant an apple tree. Raquel had done an hour's worth of research, including a call to Tía Enriqueta in Casas Grandes, and all her sources agreed that early in the spring, or even later that fall, would be better. She didn't want to wait that long, though.

Besides, maybe what was normal didn't matter so much anymore.

Dad had to call four different nurseries before he finally managed to find a sapling. Now the tree sat, ready to be planted, in a black plastic container behind the cash register at the farm stand. Raquel pressed her finger into the soil to make sure it wasn't too dry, then checked the time on her phone—4:47. Dad and Lu were two minutes late.

"They probably got stuck behind a train in Stockton," Jules said. "That always happens when I have track meets down there." She carried a basket of summer squash to an empty space on one of the produce tables.

"Yeah, probably," Raquel mumbled.

She turned to the small glass jars of jam she was supposed to be organizing. They were Sylvia's latest recipes—sour cherry and almond, and raspberry-jalapeño. Her eyes wandered from their labels to the wall above the cash register, where two new frames hung alongside the old black-and-white picture of the original farm stand.

One was a wedding photo, not from the official photographer, but a selfie Raquel had snapped right after the vows when Tía Enriqueta had draped the lazo over Dad's and Sylvia's shoulders as a symbol of togetherness and new beginnings. Instead of rosary beads, the lazo was made of flowers from the ranch, and before the minister could continue with the ceremony, Jules ducked underneath the garland, too, pulling Raquel and Lucinda along behind her until they all stood together inside the circle of roses. Sylvia said the picture—and the potpourri Jules and Lu had made out of the dried flower petals—were the best wedding presents she received.

Inside the other frame was a printout of a travel story.

SECRET INGREDIENTS:
AT THIS NORTHERN MEXICO RANCH,
DISCOVER THE UNTOLD STORY BEHIND
A TREASURED CONFECTION
By Raquel Mendoza

It was her interview with Tía Enriqueta, reprinted with permission, of course. When Sylvia first read it— after she wiped the tears off her cheeks—she offered to put Raquel in touch with an editor she'd worked with in the past. "No promises," Sylvia had warned. "She's tough. But she'll give you good feedback."

It took what felt like a hundred rounds of revision, but the editor eventually called Raquel to say she wanted to publish the story. She even hired a photographer to take pictures of Tía Enriqueta at Flor de Manzana.

Sylvia, sweeping some flakes of garlic skin that had fluttered onto the farm stand floor, caught Raquel re-reading the story. "Elena told me they're booked for the next two months, and everyone who calls to make a reservation mentions your piece."

It wasn't the reason she wrote it, but Raquel was glad she could be a part of telling the story—Tía Enriqueta's story—especially if it helped the ranch keep going.

And earlier that afternoon, Raquel had found out that yet another good thing had come out of the interview. But she was saving the news until everyone was around to hear it. She checked the time again—4:55.

She started a text message to Lu. *You said 4:45! Where are—*

"You don't have to send that—we're here," Lu said. "And we're hardly even late."

Raquel stuck the phone in her pocket. "I wasn't going

to send anything," she said. "Are you late? I didn't notice."

Jules snorted.

"Sorry, mija," Dad said. "We got stuck—"

"Behind a train in Stockton?" Raquel interrupted. "I figured. But now that you're here, there's something I've been wanting to tell you. All of you."

"Can I go change first?" Lu asked. "I'm pretty sweaty."

She had to be kidding. "No!" Raquel snapped.

"All right, all right," Lu said. She turned over an empty bucket and sat down on it. "Tell us, then."

Dad leaned against the counter, and Sylvia stood next to him.

"Well," Raquel started. "You know how I sent Ms. King my story about Tía Enriqueta and the ranch and the obleas and the secret recipe?"

Jules set down the crate of squash. Sylvia put a hand on her hip.

"Yes?" she said. "And ..."

"And she loved it!" Raquel said. "She wants me to co-edit the *Mirror* next year *and* she asked if I would lead a special workshop about interviews!"

Sylvia's arms were already wrapped tight around her. Raquel wriggled one hand free to meet Jules's high five.

"I'm proud of you, mija," Dad said. "But I'm not surprised."

Lu wrinkled her nose. *"Co-edit?* Does that mean you have to work with Paul Campos? Are you sure you want to?"

If Ms. King had asked at the beginning of the summer, Raquel would have refused. Well, not at first. First she would have made Ms. King listen to all the reasons *she* should be the sole editor in chief. Because if she wasn't the editor, then what was she?

But now she thought it might be interesting to have someone to share ideas with. After reading the *Mirror* all summer, she could admit that at least some of Paul's stories weren't *completely* terrible.

"Ms. King said the club needs my experience, and that with Paul around, maybe I can let go of some of the work."

Even Dad laughed at that.

"I'm almost sorry I won't be there to see it," Lu said.

"You could always change your mind," Raquel said. She was partly teasing, but partly not.

After the wedding—and several days of video calls with Mom—Lu had decided to try homeschooling. She had actually enjoyed online classes and wasn't looking forward to fighting her way through the crowded hallways at Manzanita Middle School again. She'd be able to spend more time in Lockeford, she had argued. And, most of all, she wouldn't have to give up the skate team, where she had made real friends—friends who hadn't been Raquel's first.

Even after a week, Raquel wasn't used to the idea. She knew that if she asked, Lu would go back with her. She might even rejoin the *Mirror.*

But she also knew it was too big a sacrifice. Like the kind Tía Enriqueta's grandfather had asked her to make.

"I promise I'll read it every week," Lu said.

"You better," Raquel said, hoping her smile didn't look as forced as it felt right then. "Because I'm going to quiz you." She wasn't joking.

"Well," Sylvia said, untying her apron. "I think this

calls for a celebration." To Sylvia, *everything* called for a celebration.

"I suggest blackberry cobbler," Jules said. It was the peak of the harvest, and there were more berries than Sylvia could turn into jams or Jules could use in her dyes.

"Mmm." Dad nodded. "With ice cream."

Raquel lifted the plastic container off the ground and dropped it on the counter. What were they going to do without her keeping everyone on track around here?

"First we need to plant this apple tree," she insisted. "We put it off yesterday because it was too hot, and the day before because it got too late. I'm going back home tomorrow, so it has to be *now*."

Sylvia reached under the counter for a pair of gardening gloves. "She's right, Marcos," she said, slipping the gloves on. "We better do this."

"I'll get a shovel," he agreed.

A customer looked up from a basket of strawberries. "Are you going to be selling your own apples?" she asked.

"Not yet," Raquel said. "But who knows? Maybe someday."

She picked up the tree in both arms, then led her family out of the farm stand and toward the spot she had picked out between two oaks.

It wasn't an orchard. There wouldn't be fruit for another two years at least. Even then, no one could say how much would be sweet and how much would be sour. But it was the start of something new, something to take root, something they had planted together.

Acknowledgments

First and forever, I am grateful to my grandfather Valdemar Espinoza, whose memories of his childhood in Casas Grandes inspired the setting of this book. He did not live long enough to see it published, but his stories and his love endure.

It has been such a special thing to write about a family finding their way toward a new kind of normal as I—and so many others—have been working to do the same. I could not have done it without the support of agent Jennifer Laughran; the vision and heart of editor Tiffany

Colón; the talent of illustrator Xochitl Cornejo; and the care and dedication of everyone at Scholastic, including Melissa Schirmer, Stephanie Yang, and the entire publicity and marketing teams. I am so lucky to be able to work with you.

And finally, no recipe would be complete without David, Alice, and Soledad. Thank you for the joy and inspiration you stir into our days.

About the Author

Jennifer Torres is the author of *Stef Soto, Taco Queen*; *The Fresh New Face of Griselda*; and other books for young readers. She writes stories about home, friendship, and unexpected courage inspired by her Mexican American heritage. Jennifer started her career as a newspaper reporter, and even though she writes fiction now, she hopes her stories still have some truth in them. She lives with her family in Southern California.